THE FOOTBALL GIRL

THE FOOTBALL GIRL

THATCHER HELDRING

DELACORTE PRESS

Text copyright © 2017 by Thatcher Heldring
Jacket art © 2017 Shutterstock/Selenit

All rights reserved. Published in the United States by
Delacorte Press, an imprint of Random House Children's Books,
a division of Penguin Random House LLC, New York.

Delacorte Press is a registered trademark and the colophon
is a trademark of Penguin Random House LLC.

randomhouseteens.com

Educators and librarians, for a variety of teaching tools,
visit us at RHTeachersLibrarians.com

Library of Congress Cataloging-in-Publication Data is available upon request.
ISBN 978-0-385-74183-5 (hc) — ISBN 978-0-375-98714-4 (ebook)

The text of this book is set in 12-point Fairfield.
Interior design by Heather Kelly

Printed in the United States of America
10 9 8 7 6 5 4 3 2
First Edition

For Jack,
my football boy

X X X X X

CHAPTER ONE

TESSA

SUNDAY, MAY 8

It was the day of the Pilchuck Scramble, the biggest trail run in town. I signed up as a team with my two best friends when we heard it was open to everyone. Marina, Lexie, and I were fourteen, so we were in the youngest age bracket for women. With five hundred yards to go, the runner ahead of me was fighting the trail, breathing harder, glancing over her shoulder. A few steps in front of her, the race leader was just reaching the top of the last hill. Marina and Lexie were right behind me, trying to keep the same pace.

"Showtime," I said to myself as we came to the last straightaway. In a burst of speed, I flew past the second-place runner, with Marina right on my heels. Now we were second and third. Out of the corner of my eye, I saw Lexie get caught in traffic as the other racers surged forward on the narrow path. She hadn't done anything wrong. It could have happened to any of us. That was why it was important to have three of us in the race. We won as a team or lost as a team.

I shortened my stride, picking up my pace, and took over first place as the finish chute came into view. I saw the look of shock as I breezed past my latest victim. She seemed to lose heart, and her pace fell just enough for Marina to dart into second, right behind me. And that was how we finished.

After the race, Marina, Lexie, and I posed arm in arm in arm for a million photos, mostly taken by Marina's mom. When we finally had a moment to ourselves, we high-fived and hugged. Marina hosed me with her water bottle while Lexie laughed like crazy, so I doused her back. We were drenched when a woman in a Pilchuck High School cross-country shirt came up to us.

"Congratulations, girls," she said.

"Thanks," we all said at once.

"You three make a great team. How long have you been running together?"

"Since sixth grade," I said. "We all go to the Rosemary School."

"We're going to Pilchuck High this fall," Marina added.

The woman smiled. "I'm Coach Harper. I hope you're thinking about cross-country in the fall."

"Definitely," said Marina.

"We're a package deal, though," Lexie explained.

"Well, I could picture all of you being in my top seven,"

Coach Harper said. "You'll have to earn it, but I like what I see."

"She loves us," Marina said after Coach Harper had left.

"Top seven," Lexie repeated, savoring the words. "We'll actually be able to win races—as *freshmen*."

While Marina and Lexie were celebrating, I was looking across the park at a group of boys playing a game of two-hand-touch football. About a year ago I had started playing pickup with the boys on my street. Now we were on a flag football team together, something I didn't talk too much about with Marina and Lexie. I was afraid they would think it was weird. After all, there were no other girls playing football in Pilchuck.

"Tessa," Marina said to me, "isn't this awesome?"

"It's the best," I said, trying to be enthusiastic.

Marina and Lexie gave each other a look.

"What?" I asked.

"Tessa, it's obvious you're dying to go over there," Marina replied.

"It is?"

Lexie nodded. "We can see you staring."

"Do you mind?" I asked. "I just want to say hi."

"Suuure," Marina answered. "On one condition: you need to tell us which one of them is the lucky boy."

I did my best to laugh it off. "Oh, he's just my neighbor," I said, trying not to blush. "His name is Caleb. You know him, right? He goes to Riverside." He was another one of my secrets.

"We've seen him around," Lexie said. "So when are you going to introduce us?"

"Soon," I said. "I promise."

After one more quick round of high fives and hugs, I said goodbye and walked over to the football game. I was a bit relieved when my friends didn't try to follow me. I loved them, but I wanted to keep football and Caleb to myself a little while longer.

Chapter Two

→ CALEB

Aaron Parker stood in the middle of the field clutching a football as he pleaded with Brian Braun not to leave. "If you bail, we're down to nine," Aaron said. "We'll have uneven teams."

"Sorry, man," Brian answered. "It's Sunday. I gotta work."

"One more drive," Aaron said.

"Can't do it," Brian responded before jogging away.

I had hoped Brian would change his mind. I didn't want the game to end. Even though it was just two-hand-touch, it was a big deal to me, and to my friends Nick and Dobie, to be on the field with Aaron and Brian. We were eighth graders, and they were starters on the varsity football team at Pilchuck High. Brian was the quarterback and Aaron was the middle linebacker, like my brother Charlie had been before he'd graduated two years ago. It was Charlie who had gotten me, Nick, and Dobie into the game today.

"It's cool," Charlie said to Aaron. "I'll play quarterback both ways."

Aaron looked disappointed, but I knew he wouldn't argue with Charlie. Charlie had taught him everything about playing middle linebacker. "Okay," Aaron said reluctantly. "Let's try it."

I was a little bummed too because I'd been playing quarterback that afternoon and had gotten into a rhythm. With Nick blocking and Dobie running the ball, we'd held our own against Aaron, Brian, and the other high school players. Of course, having Charlie on our team had helped. We switched the game to four-on-four with a permanent QB, but it wasn't the same. It was hard to stay competitive when one of the players was on both teams.

That was when Tessa Dooley appeared. She was wearing running shorts and a long-sleeved T-shirt. A medal hung around her neck. Tessa and I went to different schools, but I had known her forever. The Dooleys lived down the street, and Tessa used to join our games of street football. Earlier this year she joined our flag team. She and I started hanging out more this spring, doing homework at the library and playing *Madden* at my house. Now when I saw her, my pulse quickened and my hands got all clammy. I wasn't sure what it meant, but it felt like a good thing.

I pulled Nick and Dobie aside. "Let's ask Tessa if she wants to join."

"I don't know, man," Dobie said. "You bring a girl in, it changes things."

"We already know she can play," I replied.

"And it beats playing with a permanent QB," Nick added.

"He's got a point," I said to Dobie, knowing I would have to say something to Tessa before too long.

Dobie looked at Aaron. I knew what he was thinking. Maybe *we* knew Tessa could play, but to the older guys she was just a girl.

We were still debating when Charlie waved at Tessa. "You want in?"

Tessa pointed at herself. "Me?"

Aaron glanced at Charlie but didn't say anything.

Charlie nodded. "Yeah. We need one more. Come on."

Quickly Tessa pulled off her medal and dropped it in the grass. She ran onto the field. "What team am I on?"

"Over here," Aaron said to Tessa.

"Hey," Charlie said. "Next score wins."

Aaron nodded as he waited for Tessa. She was at least a foot shorter than anyone else in the game and disappeared behind her teammates as she joined them in the huddle.

When her team came to the line of scrimmage, Tessa was standing directly across from me. "Get ready, McCleary," she said. "The ball's coming to me."

"Is that a challenge?" I asked, unable to stop myself from smirking.

"It's a promise," she answered with a straight face, looking at Jose, who was playing QB.

Jose snapped the ball to himself, and Tessa darted forward, then juked right, crossing the field on a slant route.

She lost me in the crowd. Jose spotted her and rifled the ball in Tessa's direction, but she didn't get her hands up fast enough. Incomplete.

"Gotta catch those," Aaron said.

"Okay," Tessa answered.

On second down, Tessa tried to beat me on a post route. She was fast, but I kept up with her. Jose moved his team downfield with three straight completions to Aaron.

"We should double Parker," Dobie said in the huddle.

"You want to play a zone?" Nick asked.

Dobie shook his head. "Nah, I'm just thinking Caleb can help Charlie out on Aaron. We don't really need to guard Tessa."

"Are you sure?" I said. "She can catch."

"I'll take my chances," Dobie said.

"What do you think?" I asked Charlie.

"It's worth a shot," Charlie replied with his arm around my shoulder. "Drop back like a free safety and help me with Aaron. But keep an eye on Tessa. If Jose does throw to her, you'll need to hustle."

I did what Charlie had said. Tessa ran a shallow curl while Aaron headed straight for the end zone. I saw Jose look Aaron's way, and I ran over to back up Charlie. Jose pumped, then pulled the ball back. He whipped a short pass to Tessa, who caught the ball, turned, and raced to the goal line. Dobie took a smart angle and cut her off, leaving her with nowhere to run. But instead of stepping out-of-bounds, Tessa tried to pitch the ball backward to Aaron, who wasn't ready. The ball bounced off his hip and hit the ground. Charlie scooped it up and ran twenty yards before Jose tagged him near midfield.

"What was that?" Aaron asked.

"Sorry, bad idea," Tessa answered. She had lost her swagger.

Charlie called for a water break between possessions, and I walked over to her. "Don't worry about it," I said.

"Thanks." Tessa sighed. "I think I'm a little nervous."

"You?" I asked. I wasn't sure I'd ever seen Tessa nervous.

"Hey, I'm human. And these guys are, like, real football players."

"Gee, thanks," I said.

"You know what I mean," Tessa replied. "They throw hard." Suddenly she brightened. Touching my wrist, she added, "Ask me later about the race."

Just then Aaron called his team together. "All right," he said. "Let's stop 'em." He looked at Tessa. "You take him," Aaron said, pointing at Nick.

Charlie handed me the ball. "Hey," he added with a smile. "Do you realize you're about to lead a game-winning drive against the starting middle linebacker and four of his friends?"

"Are you trying to jinx me?"

"Can't jinx greatness," he replied.

On first down, I threaded a ball over Aaron's hands to Dobie for eight yards. Next I baited Jose into blitzing me after a ten-Mississippi count, dodged his tag, and ran for another fifteen yards. The defense tightened in the red zone, and I couldn't find an open receiver. On the third down,

I scrambled for a few more yards. Suddenly we had one play left.

"What do you want to do?" Charlie asked me.

"They're going to come after you again," Dobie said. "Let's set up a screen."

"Too risky," Charlie answered. "If we don't get into the end zone, drive's over."

"How about this?" I said. "Charlie and Dobie line up left. They'll overload. I'll roll out and hit one of you crossing the field."

"You're going to throw a ball to the end zone across your body while rolling away from the receiver?" Nick asked. "Good luck."

"I can do it."

At first, the play went like I thought it would. But Charlie and Dobie couldn't shake their coverage. Aaron smelled blood and came at me. He reached out with two hands. I ducked but felt my foot slide. I lost my balance, then caught myself just before my knee hit the ground. Aaron was charging me. There was a mad-dog look in his eyes. I had a feeling this game was no longer two-hand-touch. Suddenly he was airborne, flying at me like a missile. In the end zone, Charlie had a half step on Jose. It was enough. I gunned the ball into his hands for the game winner just as all two hundred pounds of Aaron Parker slammed into me. Spitting dirt, I jumped up and ran toward Charlie, pumping my fist like we had just won the Super Bowl.

After we celebrated, I calmed down enough to worry

that I had overdone it. Had I just showed up half of the starting defense of the high school football team?

But Aaron held out his fist. "Impressive. You're definitely a McCleary."

"Thanks," I said. "Good game."

"Sorry about the hit there," Aaron added.

"I can take it."

"No doubt," Aaron answered.

Tessa came up to us. "Hey, thanks for letting me play," she said to Aaron. "That was fun."

"Anytime," he said.

"Really?" Tessa asked.

"Well, we don't do this that often," Aaron said.

"Oh sure," Tessa said. "I get it."

Aaron looked me in the eye. "See you around, McCleary."

"Definitely."

Tessa sent a smirk my way after Aaron left. "Definitely," she mimicked, obviously making fun of me for trying to sound cool. "See you around, bro," she added.

"What?" I said. "That's what people say."

"You're such a dork," she replied with a laugh.

"I'm a dork who just beat your team," I retorted.

Before Tessa could answer, a large arm wrapped itself around my neck, pulling me toward the ground. "This loser bothering you?" Charlie asked Tessa.

"Yes," she said. "And he smells weird."

"Oh, that's just me," Charlie said. Then he drove my face into his armpit. "Do I smell, loser?"

"Like a sewer," I said when Charlie released me.

"Seriously, good stuff today. Those guys were impressed. They want you on the team next year. Actually, all three of you," he said, pointing to Nick and Dobie.

"I don't know," Dobie joked. "I may try out for the debate team."

"You couldn't make the spelling team," Nick added.

"That makes no sense," Dobie said.

"Neither does your being on the debate team."

"But at least the debate team is a real thing," Dobie shot back.

While Dobie and Nick went at it, Tessa and I agreed to go to the Pilchuck Market for drinks. I was walking on air as we made our way out of Boardman Park.

Chapter Three

→TESSA

I was proud of myself for joining the pickup game. Maybe even prouder than I had been of winning the Pilchuck Scramble. Caleb had been so nice to me the entire time. And, wow, what an arm. The boy could throw. I wondered how he thought I had played.

"So what does it feel like to get hit like that?" I asked.

"It wakes you up."

"Does it hurt?"

"Nothing I can't handle," Caleb replied.

"Nothing I can't handle, bro," I imitated, teasing him.

"First of all," Caleb said as we waited at an intersection for the walk sign, "that's not what I sound like. And when do I ever say *bro*?"

"Okay," I said. "I'll stop."

We crossed Verlot Street and went into the store. I picked up a water bottle and a protein bar while Caleb got peanut butter M&M's. We found a table and sat down. *Tell me I played well*, I begged silently. *Tell me I played well*.

"Oh, hey, I almost forgot," Caleb said.

Yes? I thought, ready to be showered with compliments.

But Caleb wasn't picking up on my vibe. "You were going to tell me about the race," he said.

"Right, the race. It's not really a big deal or anything. My friends and I received medals in the trail run. For our group winning first place in our age bracket."

"Cool. Can I see the medal?"

I reached down to show Caleb the shiny gold circle I'd hung around my neck. It took me less than a second to realize I had left it lying in the grass in the middle of the field in Boardman Park.

"Oh no," I said, patting myself frantically up and down as if the medal might magically appear. "I didn't. I didn't." I looked over at Caleb. "I did. I lost my medal. I took it off before the game and I left it there."

I pictured my poor medal lying alone in the rain (even though it wasn't raining), and it made me sad. Then I imagined Lexie and Marina at home with their medals and it made me even sadder. They'd be so disappointed in me—the irresponsible one who couldn't even keep track of a medal.

"Let's go look for it," Caleb said.

"I can't. I have to get home. My parents are waiting for me. It's . . . my birthday," I said hesitantly, not wanting to make a big deal out of it.

"Today's your birthday? That's awesome. Did you get anything good?"

"I got a medal," I said pathetically.

"You'll get it back," Caleb promised as though there wasn't a doubt in his mind.

"I hope so," I answered.

Caleb wished me happy birthday as we headed for home. He walked me to my driveway, where he wished me happy birthday again before he left. I made my way to the door, trying to imagine what Mom and Dad had gotten me. In my dreams it was new bedroom furniture, a laptop, headphones, cash. I would have unwrapped any of those happily. But I knew my parents would not gift me what I wanted. They would get me what they wanted to give me. Big difference.

My dog, Oreo, greeted me at the front door. I scratched him under his chin, dropped my bag, and wandered into the kitchen. Our kitchen was a large open space with lots of light and an L-shaped island in the middle that was always covered with papers and calendars. Past the kitchen was the living room, where we had two big couches facing each other and a coffee table in between.

I saw Mom and Dad sitting on the couches. Something large, flat, and square wrapped in butcher paper was leaning against the coffee table.

"There she is," Mom said, like I was a package she'd been waiting for the mailman to deliver.

"Happy birthday, honey," Dad said. "How was your day?"

"Good," I said, nibbling on a carrot I'd found in the

refrigerator. "I came in first in my age group. We got medals. But mine is lying in the grass in the park."

"That's wonderful, Tessa," Dad said. "Good for you."

"You lost your medal?" Mom asked.

"Well, I didn't lose it. I know where it is. I just don't have it with me right now."

"Tessa, I wish you'd be more responsible."

Suddenly I knew what I wanted for my birthday. A time machine so I could go back thirty seconds and erase the moment when I'd mentioned the medal. I should have known Mom would miss the part about me winning the race and obsess about me forgetting the medal.

"I would have gone to get it, but you said I was supposed to come home right after. What do you want?"

"We just want you to be successful," Mom replied. Not a bit sorry for having missed a great race. Expectation of a win: met. Expectation of being a responsible adult: not met. Time for Mom to act. "And that starts with being responsible."

I took a deep breath, closed the refrigerator door, and looked at my parents in the living room. Mom was gazing into space. The look on her face was a mixture of deep concern (probably about my academic future) and irritating satisfaction (because she was going to be the one to solve all my problems). Dad was glancing sideways at his phone like the message that came through next would determine the fate of the planet, unless he missed it. Best birthday party *ever*. I didn't know why I was disappointed. This was exactly what I'd expected. I hadn't had a birthday party thrown for me since I was five years old.

"So, what's the big surprise?" I asked.

Now Mom was back, totally focused on the moment. It happened so quickly, and she was smiling so broadly, I knew right away that whatever was wrapped up in the living room was about her.

"Go ahead, Alan," Mom said, gesturing to the package.

"Wait. I don't even get to open my own present?"

"Well, it's not a present exactly," Dad explained. We made eye contact just long enough for him to send an urgent message, *I'm sorry for this, Tessa. I'll make it up to you.*

"It's very exciting," Mom added.

"I can't wait," I said, crossing the threshold from the kitchen into the living room so that I had a front-row seat for the unwrapping.

Dad began to rip off the paper.

"Carefully," Mom said.

A moment later, I knew the big surprise.

And it wasn't a surprise at all.

Chapter Four

→ CALEB

MONDAY, MAY 9

I was standing in the courtyard at school when Dobie drove his shoulder into mine, propelling me forward. Luckily, I managed to still hold on to my cell phone.

Dobie was built tough but was shorter than me. We'd become friends in elementary school, but since the beginning of this year, he had been changing. His hair was longer, he had an earring, and his grades were even worse than mine. My mom complained that his T-shirts were satanic. No matter what he looked like, though, Dobie and I still had one thing in common. We loved football.

"Who are you texting?" he asked.

"Nobody," I said.

"Tessa?"

"Yeah."

"You like her?"

"Kinda."

"That's cool."

I put my phone into my pocket. "Where's Nick?" I asked.

"That nerd?" Dobie questioned. "Probably getting extra credit."

Just then our phones buzzed at the same time.

Dobie read his message out loud.

Verlot Street bridge, 10:00. Friday AP.

"Same here," I said. "Who's AP?"

Dobie shrugged. "No idea. Ariel, Amanda, Amy?"

"You're as dumb as you look. You think there's a girl who wants to meet you at a bridge at ten on a Friday night?"

Suddenly Nick appeared from the crowd. "You guys get this?" he asked, holding up his phone.

"Okay, I guess it's not from a girl," Dobie said grimly.

"Do you know who AP is?" I asked.

"Just think about it," Nick said. "What happens every spring on the Verlot Street bridge?"

I snapped my fingers. "The plunge."

The plunge was a secret Pilchuck tradition—the kind you only knew about if you needed to. Every spring, older players on the high school football team dared a group of eighth graders to jump off the Verlot Street bridge. My brother Charlie had done it when he was in eighth grade. Now it was my turn. A lump started to form at the base of my throat.

Dobie's eyes opened wide. "AP, dude."

Nick nodded. "Aaron Parker."

"So this is real," I said.

Dobie nodded confidently. "It's real. Just like we always said."

Nick got quiet.

"What's wrong with you?" Dobie asked.

"The bridge," Nick answered. "Have you ever looked over the side? It's high."

"Don't worry about it," I said. "Charlie told me they've been doing the plunge since my dad was our age, and nobody's ever gotten hurt."

"Really?" Nick asked.

"Yeah," Dobie said. "I mean, except for that one time."

"Oh right," I said, playing along. "Did they ever find that guy?"

"Just an arm floating down the river."

Nick swung his backpack at Dobie. "Pond turd," he said.

Dobie ducked, then jumped onto Nick's back. "You missed me," he said. "Just don't miss the river."

I pulled Dobie off Nick. "Can we eat?" I said. "I'm hungry."

We hit Pilchuck Market on the way home from school. Nick got a hot dog. Dobie loaded up on fries. I grabbed an apple and a Gatorade. We sat at one of the plastic tables out front and chowed.

"You're not going to eat anything?" Dobie asked me. He looked me in the eye. "What, are you afraid of the plunge?"

"It's a long way down to the river," I said.

"It's not the river we have to worry about," Dobie replied with an evil smile. "It's the rocks."

"Oh great," said Nick. "So either we drown or we hit a boulder face-first at fifty miles an hour."

Dobie looked at Nick. "More like a hundred miles an hour for you," he said.

"Breaking news, stupid," Nick answered. "Weight has nothing to do with how fast an object falls."

"I know it's a tradition," I said, "but I wish we didn't have to do it." The gnawing fear that had showed up when we'd realized it was time for the plunge was back.

"Here we go again," Dobie said.

"What are you talking about?" I asked.

"Oh, come on," said Dobie. "Every time we have a chance to do something fun, you turn into this giant blubbering chicken and try to get out of it, but you always do it anyway, so can you just do us all a favor and skip to the part where you man up and go with it? Because we all know you will. Nick, back me up."

"He's kind of right," Nick agreed reluctantly.

"So maybe I don't love doing things that are illegal and dangerous," I said. "We still don't know what this has to do with football."

"We have to prove we want to be on the team," Dobie said. "Otherwise, everyone would try out and there'd be, like, two hundred people on the roster."

"I don't think you understand how tryouts work," I said.

"Whatever, Boy Scout," murmured Dobie.

"I'm not a Boy Scout, dude. I never have been."

"Just say you're going to do it, man," Dobie pleaded. "You don't want to be the one guy who doesn't show up. They'll never let you forget it."

"Please," I said. "That wouldn't happen."

"It happened to Oliver Watts," Nick said.

"Who?" I asked.

"You never heard of the Big O?" Nick asked. "He went to our school ten or maybe twenty years ago. He was like a one-man offensive line. I'm talking two hundred and eighty pounds as a tenth grader, and quick. Total bulldozer."

"This sounds made up."

"It's all true," Nick said. "You can look it up."

"Fine. What happened to the Big O?" I asked.

"He made the team and basically carried them all season. But off the field, it was like he didn't exist. Sat alone. Dressed alone. Ate alone. Picture it. This guy is the best player on the team, maybe ever, but he's completely iced out by everyone else. All because he didn't jump."

"Tragic," Dobie said.

"He had to transfer schools," Nick added.

"Don't be the Big O, Caleb. It's not worth it."

I got Dobie's point. But the real reason I wouldn't chicken out wasn't the Big O. It was my big brother. He had jumped, and now so would I.

CHAPTER FIVE

→ TESSA

JANE DOOLEY FOR MAYOR

That was what the sign had said.

That had been the big surprise.

Happy birthday to me.

"I still can't believe you want to be mayor," I said Monday after school, settling onto one of the barstools at the island in the kitchen.

It wasn't a total surprise. Mom had been on the city council for five years, and I had heard her and Dad talking about taking the next step. I guessed this was it.

"I'm going to be mayor," Mom replied with certainty.

I grabbed a tangerine from the bowl on the counter and peeled it. I bet a lot of people in my shoes would have been thinking, *Cool. My mom's going to be mayor. Maybe I'll be on TV, or more people will want to be my friend, or I'll be able to pull some strings for anything my friends and I want to do.*

But I was having a hard time getting to *cool*. It wasn't like I was afraid this was going to change my life. My mother had been in politics since I was little. But I was concerned about our family dictator gaining even more power. And it really bugged me that my mom and dad were basically making this my birthday present.

So, maybe I sounded a little defensive. "Why are you doing this?"

"Your mom believes it's time for a change in Pilchuck," Dad said, putting his arm around Mom. "We need new leadership, someone who can help our town reach its full potential."

"Okay, that's great. But why now?"

Mom sat on the barstool next to me, making this a one-on-one conversation as Dad watched from the background. "Tessa, I've been a city councilwoman for five years. I would be a good mayor. I'm ready for this. I want this. And I'm honestly concerned about this town's priorities. So I'm running. And I hope you can be excited for me. Because it's going to take all of us."

I popped slices of tangerine into my mouth while Mom explained what she stood for.

"Number one," she said. "Sustainable growth. We can't keep building houses all over the mountain when we have open space within the city limits."

"We know that a lot of people feel the same way," Dad added.

"Number two," Mom continued. "Roads and bridges. They're in terrible shape."

"We have to fix them," Dad said.

"Number three," Mom went on. "Schools. We have to invest more in teachers, books, and other things that really matter to your education."

"Who could argue with that?" I asked, playing along.

"It's not quite that easy," Dad answered. "Finding money for one thing usually means taking it away from something else. In this case, your mom—well, we are proposing diverting funds from the new football stadium."

I knew right away that that was going to be a problem. There were a lot of football fans in Pilchuck. I had heard people my age and their parents talking about how great it would be to replace the run-down stadium where the high school team had played for years. "What do you have against football?" I asked.

"I don't have anything against football," Mom said. "Except that it's dangerous. And I think we need to prioritize education over sports. Nobody ever reached their full potential through football."

"You know I play football, right?" I asked, even though it was only flag football with Caleb and his friends. I kind of thought Caleb and those guys let me play because I was the only girl who wanted to and because I was a pretty good receiver.

"You don't play in a stadium, sweetie," Mom replied.

It might not have been in a stadium, but it was a big deal to me. We were in a league, and we were two wins away from a championship. Not that my parents cared or knew anything about the games I played in with Caleb and his friends. Mom and Dad made excuses every single time for not coming to the games. I knew they had no interest.

But any daughter of Jane Dooley's knew for sure that there was only one reason to play: to win.

"My team is in the play-offs," I said. "We have a game on Saturday."

"Oh, Tessa," Dad said, like he was devastated that he would miss the game. "I wish we'd known sooner. We have media training that day."

"What's media training?" I asked.

"Long hours with someone who thinks they know more than I do about talking to reporters," Mom said. "The trainer comes to the campaign office and tells me what to do when I'm being interviewed so that I don't say the wrong thing and embarrass myself."

"That sounds way less fun than football," I said.

"It's not that bad," Dad replied. "We're sorry we can't be at your game, but I think we'll have a lot of family time this summer."

"Please explain," I said.

Mom smiled. "Well, running for mayor is a lot of work, and I'm going to need all the help I can get. Your dad is helping with the campaign, and I want you to help me too."

"Help how?"

"There's a thousand ways," Dad said. "Making signs, knocking on doors, stuffing envelopes, waving signs."

"Anything else with signs?" I asked.

"Tessa, we're serious," Mom said. "This is a team effort. Think of it like a summer job."

"So I get paid?"

"Think of it like an internship," Dad replied. "Unless you have something more important to do," he added with an annoying wink.

I decided to pretend that I didn't know Dad was kidding. "Well, there's running with Lexie and Marina. The cross-country coach told us to keep training all summer." I looked at Mom and Dad, hoping that this one fact would make them see that I had my own life and couldn't just drop everything to work on the campaign. All I got was silence. So, I kept going. "And I have football."

"Tessa," Mom said. "Football is a free-time activity you can do with your friends. You need to think beyond summer. You are starting high school. The choices you make now are going to impact you for the rest of your life. Working on the campaign will open so many doors for you. In a few years, you could be an assistant in the mayor's office, and then, someday, maybe you're helping me run for Congress."

How had this happened? Two minutes before, I'd been an eighth grader peeling a tangerine, and now I was trying to get Mom elected to Congress? It was too much. They'd never needed my help before. They just ignored me as long as I met all their expectations. Why did they need my help for this campaign? I'd been doing fine leading my own life outside their work-obsessed ones. Now Mom had planned out my whole future without asking me. I needed to escape.

Mom and Dad went back to their laptops, and I reached for my phone. Luckily, talking with me had wasted too much of their time. Back to work.

I had to tell someone about the craziness that was going on at the Dooley house. I started to call Marina, then stopped. Marina wouldn't get it. She would listen for a few seconds and then switch the subject to something that interested her more. She definitely wouldn't understand why it was such a big deal that Mom was against the new football stadium. And Lexie would be overjoyed by the fact that my mother was running for mayor, popularity thoughts instantly floating through her head. Also, I didn't want them to know I'd lost my medal.

I knew who would get me. So I sent a message to Caleb, wondering what it meant when I needed to share this news with him rather than my best friends.

Chapter Six

CALEB

FRIDAY, MAY 13

Dobie was getting impatient. "Dude, will you hurry up?" he said, shining the light from his headlamp into my eyes. "We're going to be late. Nick's already there, and he says they're waiting for us."

"I'm going as fast as I can," I said. "These rocks are slippery. And it's dark." How had I let Dobie talk me into this?

I could have been home watching baseball or lifting with Charlie and our younger brother, Luke. Instead I was scrambling up the west bank of the Pilchuck River toward the underside of the Verlot Street bridge, where we were meeting Nick, a couple of other eighth graders, and a bunch of guys from the high school football team.

Part of me was excited. Only a few eighth graders every year had the chance to be a part of the plunge. If I survived, it would be something Charlie and I would always have in common. He would be proud of me, and that meant a lot. Still, I was scared. "This is crazy," I said when I reached the top of the bank. It was now a short dash to the bridge, which was busy with cars, even though it was night. We'd have to stay out of sight.

"What's crazy?" Dobie asked. "This is fun. You gotta lighten up. Live a little."

Dobie was right. I wasn't much of a risk-taker. I didn't like the idea of getting in trouble or cracking my head on a rock in the river. I was the good son, the one who never got in trouble and always followed the rules. But I also hated being left out.

"Hey," I whispered. "Isn't there a rule that you shouldn't jump off a bridge just because someone else did it?"

"Yeah," Dobie replied. "Unless you're asked by Brian Braun and Aaron Parker."

We reached the bridge undetected.

"Up there," I said, pointing to a wide metal beam, where Nick and the other eighth graders were standing and staring into the darkness.

Bolted to the underside of the bridge was a very large sign that said NO TRESPASSING. VIOLATORS WILL BE PROSECUTED.

Dobie and I climbed up to the beam and shuffled out to the middle so that we were over the deepest part of the river.

"Get ready to jump," Brian ordered.

I closed my eyes and tried to remember what Charlie had told me. Charlie had done the same jump and survived. Point your toes down. Keep your arms at your side. Watch out for the rocks. Charlie was the one who had ultimately convinced me that I needed to do this. He'd said football wasn't just about making the team. Almost anyone could do that. It was about being a part of the team. According to Charlie, jumping off the bridge was a tradition and an honor, and I would understand why when it was all over.

"One," said Brian.

"Man, that's a long way down," Dobie muttered.

"Two."

"We'll be fine," I promised him.

"Thr—"

"I CAN'T DO IT!"

We couldn't tell who had panicked. It wasn't me, or Dobie, or Nick. But whoever it was had yelled loudly enough to be heard over the traffic on the bridge. Suddenly there were voices calling over the rail, faces looking to the water below.

"What's going on down there?"

"It's a group of kids!"

"They're jumping!"

"JUMP!" was the last thing I heard Brian say before he leapt into the river. Aaron was in the air right after him.

There was nowhere to run. People were everywhere, on both sides of the bridge. We had two choices.

"See ya," Dobie said.

I watched him drop into the water.

"Lord save me," Nick muttered.

And he was gone.

"You need to come off the bridge now," someone said. "The police are on their way."

"Tell them I'm sorry," I said.

The water came so fast that I had no time to think. I was in the river, being pulled gently downstream by the current. When I broke the surface, I could see Dobie and Nick crouched behind a boulder on the bank. It was an easy swim to shore, and I quickly left the water and hid with my friends. Spotlights searched the area.

Soon we were in the thick woods that covered the hillside. Grasping roots and tree trunks, we pulled ourselves to level ground, where we sat shivering in the dark until we thought nobody was still looking for us.

We jogged across the bridge in soggy shoes, and in the moonlight we saw two figures near a signpost. They ducked into the shadows as we approached, then reappeared when we were closer. I recognized Aaron and Brian.

"What's up?" Aaron asked. "You guys good?"

"We're good," said Dobie.

Brian stuck out his fist for Dobie. "That took guts," he said.

"What happened to the other guys?" I asked.

"Probably home hiding under their beds," Aaron replied.

"Chickens," Brian added.

Aaron nodded in agreement. "Anyway, they're out."

"Out of what?" I asked.

"Out of this," Brian answered.

"What about us?" Dobie asked.

"Don't worry about it," Aaron replied. "You guys are definitely in."

We split up a few minutes later. Aaron and Brian headed

down Verlot Street toward town. Dobie, Nick, and I went the other way toward our neighborhood. Even though it was a mild night, I was starting to shiver in my wet clothes. The high from the plunge was wearing off. Dobie and Nick continued to relive the jump like it was the most amazing thing they had ever done. Part of me envied them. Why did I have to be the only one silently stressing about what could have happened? But another part of me felt like a warrior. I had jumped. I had survived. I was in. And that felt really, really good. Charlie would be proud.

Dad was waiting in the kitchen when I slipped into the house later that night. He didn't have to ask where I'd been. He had done it, just like Charlie, and now me.

"You okay?" he asked.

"Yeah, I'm all right."

"Scared?"

The question surprised me. Dad never talked about being scared of anything, except taxes, bills, and his customers switching to concrete siding. I saw no reason to hide the truth. "A little," I admitted.

"You should be," Dad said. "Jumping off a bridge is stupid and dangerous."

"Am I in trouble?" I asked.

Dad shook his head. "Not this time," he replied. "What you did tonight was a tradition. I get that. Tradition is important. You need that as a team. But from now on, no more bridges. And don't tell your mother."

"No problem," I said, relieved.

Dad squeezed my shoulder. "Glad you're home."

"Me too," I said.

I went upstairs to my room, closed my door, changed into dry shorts, and passed out face-first on my bed. I didn't wake up until morning.

CHAPTER SEVEN
→TESSA

SATURDAY, MAY 14

The first time Caleb ever touched my hand was the day he showed me how to throw a football. We were ten. That was before I started playing flag football, before we started hanging out together whenever we had a chance, which was challenging, since we went to different schools. But the last time he touched my hand, we were walking to get doughnuts. That was last month. Now we weren't just friends. We were something more. I just wished I knew what.

I finally got to tell Caleb the whole story on Saturday morning. When I'd texted him earlier in the week, he had written back:

Whoa, you're going to be famous.

When I found him on Saturday, he was standing on the corner, looking proud. His hands were stuffed into the pocket of his hoodie.

"What is it?" I asked.

"Close your eyes," he said.

Based on what I knew about boys, I figured Caleb was either going to kiss me or shoot me in the face with a water gun. I took my chances.

"Hold out your hands," he said when my eyes were closed.

That was a twist. But I did it.

A second later something cool and metallic was resting on my palm.

I opened my eyes to see my medal.

"I found it in the park," Caleb said.

"You went back?" I asked.

"Yesterday."

"I'm going to hug you."

"Okay."

Caleb was tall enough that my head fit snugly under his chin. He had black curly hair that hung over his ears and forehead, and he was stronger than most of the other boys. That was because he had real chores, like hammering aluminum siding onto houses, a kind of muscle development completely different from the muscles you get from setting a table. He looked like he could play any sport he wanted.

After I hugged him, I noticed a big red welt on his leg.

"What happened to you?" I asked.

"I jumped off a bridge," he said with a smile.

"Ha ha. Seriously, tell me."

Caleb stopped smiling. "Seriously, I jumped off the Verlot Street bridge."

"When?"

"Last night."

"Why would you jump off a bridge into a river at night? That seems epically stupid. No offense."

Caleb shrugged. "I guess I had to."

"Why? Because everyone else did it?"

I listened as he explained the plunge and Aaron Parker and how it was a tradition for the football team and how all the men in his family had done it too.

"You're crazy," I said.

"Oh, like you wouldn't have done it," Caleb said.

"I don't do anything I don't want to do," I said. "Especially if it could get me killed. I have a mind of my own."

"So do I," Caleb answered.

I looked him in the eyes. "Doesn't seem like it."

"All right, fine," he said. "Maybe it wasn't the smartest thing I've ever done. But I survived. Now I can say I did it."

Was this what boys lived for? To defy death just so they could talk about it later? I would never understand them. As for Caleb, he really meant it that he thought he had to jump off the bridge. Like when I threw a ball for Oreo and he fetched it even if he didn't actually want to. He just wanted to make everyone happy. How could I not fall for a guy who just wanted to make everyone around him happy?

We stopped in town for bagels before our football game.

I had an everything with cream cheese. He had a plain with butter.

"I can't believe my mom is running for mayor," I said, munching on my bagel.

"Could be kind of cool, right? You'd be famous."

"Let's see if you think it's still cool after I tell you why she's running."

"You mean, like what she stands for?"

"Yeah. One is . . . I forget what one is. Two is something about bridges."

"What's three? Because so far this is pretty boring."

"Shut up. I'm getting to the good part. Number three is, she wants to take the money for the football stadium and use it toward enhancing our education. Her words, not mine."

Caleb's eyes opened a little wider. Finally a reaction. "No stadium?"

"I know, right?"

"That's crazy."

"I then mentioned to her that I play football. Which she can never remember, pretty much like everything else I do in my life," I said.

"Does she know you have a game today?"

"I told her. But I don't think she really heard me."

"My parents aren't going either. At the beginning of the season, they asked if they were supposed to go to my games. I told them to wait for the real thing. I think they were relieved."

"What makes you say that?"

"Because my dad said, 'Oh good.' They're always stressed

about the family business, so they only want to go if it's a real high school game."

Caleb smiled, and I laughed. It was comforting to know that I wouldn't be the only one without parents on the sideline. It was even better that the other person was Caleb, because it was one more thing we had in common. I squeezed his hand. "If you need to cry, I won't tell anyone."

"You rule," Caleb said.

"Tell me that after the game," I replied.

CHAPTER EIGHT

CALEB

Tessa was kind of our secret weapon. Early on in every game, the other team would cheat on defense, trying to double up on Roy or one of the other guys, which left Tessa open. And she would make them pay. By the time they figured out she was a threat, they'd be too far behind to catch up. We racked up the Ws. Now we were one win away from the championship. But word was out that Tessa was legit. Today she'd have to beat her man straight up. I wondered if she could do it.

Tessa must have been thinking the same thing. "No way I'm getting open deep," she said as we walked to the field. "It's going to be all underneath stuff."

"You're quick," I said. "Run a few slant routes. They'll figure that's all you can do. Then, BAM, give 'em a hitch and go."

"Bam," Tessa replied with a fist pump. "I like it."

"I like you too," I said.

The words hung in the air. The minute I'd said them, I wanted them back, like a quarterback who knew he had let the ball fly too soon. Did I think it was some big secret that I liked Tessa? No. She probably knew. Charlie told me girls had a sixth sense about things like that. Plus, I had bought her snacks at Pilchuck Market at least twice. But I had never actually said it. What if she freaked out? That would be bad. It would get really weird between us, and the team would need another slot receiver. "I mean, I like *it*," I corrected myself in a panic.

But Tessa cut me off. "It's too late," she replied. "You already said it to me."

We had come to a stop right on Verlot Street, near the Landover Lumber store. People were streaming past us with new gardening tools, freshly cut two-by-fours, and twenty-pound bags of wood chips.

"I was talking about football."

"Yeah, but you were thinking about me. You have to admit it now, Caleb. You like me. We're beyond friends."

She was so honest. So direct. How was she able to just come out like that and say everything that was going on? Her statement blew my mind. Like in earth science when Julian had asked what was beyond the edge of the universe and Ms. Baylor had said there was no scientific answer. What was beyond just friends? I had a feeling there was no scientific answer to that one either. I wished I could hide behind a stack of lumber long enough to call Charlie, but I didn't want to make this even more awkward. I hoped Tessa had something to say. "So, then, what are you?"

"You know," she said.

"You mean?" I asked.

She nodded slowly. I had to say, she looked very pretty in her green football jersey, long-sleeved white shirt, and gray football pants. And the eye black brought out the green in her eyes.

This was fourth and goal with no time on the clock. If I called the right play, it was all good. Tessa would be my girlfriend and we'd both know it. If I called the wrong play, it was game over. *Down-set, down-set, down-set, hike!* "Girlfriend?"

CHAPTER NINE
TESSA

And that was how Caleb became my boyfriend. I was very happy, a little relieved, kind of dizzy, and still pretty confused. I realized that even when you gave something a name, you still had to figure out what it meant. I guessed that would come next. First, though, we had a game to play.

CHAPTER TEN

→ CALEB

It was weird being on a football team with my girlfriend. It was even weirder when she played better than I did. At least for one game.

Chapter Eleven

→ TESSA

"Awesome game today, Tessa."

"You were on fire."

"Insane catch."

"Epic."

I went down the line, bumping fists one by one with each of the guys. "Thanks," I said, still clutching the football I had just caught for the game-winning touchdown.

Caleb was waiting at the end. "Bam," he said, slapping my hand. For just a second, he wrapped his long fingers around mine.

"Bam," I said back.

"Champs," he said with a smile.

"One more game," I reminded him.

"We got it," he answered confidently before Dobie and Nick pulled him aside.

I smiled to myself as I untied my cleats. Caleb had been saying those three words again and again since this season of flag football had begun two months before—way back in early March. *We got it.* He said it, and we believed it. Even when we lost, he made us think we had it. It was contagious. *He* was contagious. It was another reason I liked him so much.

I had just finished lacing up my sneakers when Lexie and Marina appeared. We had plans to go on a trail run in Boardman Park. We were now training to be shoo-ins for the top seven on the high school cross-country team in the fall.

"Nice game, Tess," said Lexie.

"You saw?" I asked.

"Just the end," Lexie replied.

"So, what were you smiling about?" Marina asked.

"I wasn't smiling."

Lexie and Marina just stared at me.

"Oh, that smile. Just thinking about the game."

Marina glanced over at Caleb, who was trying to juggle three footballs. "You know you want to tell us."

I glanced quickly over at Caleb to make sure he wasn't paying attention. Then I leaned into Marina and Lexie and let it all out. "Okay, you're right," I said. "You guys are my best friends, so you should be the first to know. I think this is for real. We're going—you know." I wasn't sure how to finish the sentence.

Lexie looked at me impatiently. "Dancing?"

"Bowling?" Marina asked.

"Out!" I snapped. "We're going out." I lowered my voice. "Caleb is my boyfriend."

"That sounds official," Marina said.

"I want you to like him," I said.

Lexie gazed casually at the boys. "Well, I've never talked to him. But he looks all right from a distance."

Marina hugged me. "Just don't forget about us."

Lexie still had her eyes on the boys. "Maybe I'll get a closer look at all his friends."

"No," Marina said, pulling her away. "We have to go."

"Okay. Wait one sec," I said quickly.

I walked over to Caleb, my now boyfriend, who had given up on juggling and was now doing something very un-athletic with the palm of his hand and his armpit. I vowed to never hold his hand again.

"You want to get some pizza?" he asked when he saw me.

"Yes," I said. "But I can't. I have to train."

"For real?"

"It's important," I said.

"What's more important than pizza with your team-mates?"

"Running with my friends so we can be the best cross-country runners Pilchuck High School has ever seen," I said with a smile.

"Come on," Caleb said. "You don't need to go running. You just ran all over the field. You need pizza."

"When I get my mile down to seven minutes, I'll eat pizza."

"Seven minutes . . . Is that good?

"Good is not my goal," I replied.

"How come you're now so serious?" he asked.

"I'm not that serious."

"Compared to me you are," he said shyly.

"I really want to make the top spot on the team, and you want to win next week, don't you?" I retorted.

"Sure I do. I told you we got it."

"I know you *think* we can win. But do you *want* to win?" I said.

Caleb held the football out in his right hand until it brushed against my left shoulder. "Trust me. I'm in it to win it. Whatever it takes."

"That's better," I said, too distracted by everything to make eye contact with Caleb. Behind him, I could see Lexie and Marina waving me over. "I gotta go. See you later."

"Bam," he said.

"Bam," I said back, thinking we had the weirdest code ever for *I like you*.

My mile that afternoon was 7:14, my best ever. I guess it was possible to turn raw emotion into speed. I didn't even want to stop. I knew Lexie and Marina felt the same way. Except I wasn't sure we were running toward the same thing. I was starting to think I needed more than a finish line for a goal. Maybe there was something bigger. I was a game away from being a part of the best flag football team in Pilchuck— and to me, that was pretty cool. After all, it wasn't every day a girl had a chance to win a football championship.

Chapter Twelve

↪ CALEB

After the game, Nick, Dobie, and I headed to town for pizza. It was cool for mid-May. We walked along the river into a breeze that felt like winter when it hit the sweat on my T-shirt. Thick clouds rolled in front of the sun as we came within sight of the athletic fields behind Pilchuck High School. That fall, we would be starting there as ninth graders.

Tessa would be there too. We had never been at the same school. I was pretty sure it was going to be great. We always had a lot to talk about. She made me laugh. I already knew she fit in with my friends. If we had class together, she might even let me copy her work. The bonus of having a smart girlfriend.

"Look at that scoreboard," said Nick. "Can you imagine our names on that screen? We're going to be huge."

"You're already huge," said Dobie.

Nick glared at Dobie through his glasses. "I was speaking

metaphorically, stupid." Nick wasn't fat, but my brother Charlie said if Nick didn't watch it, he would be, because all the muscle in his arms and chest would turn to flab.

Dobie looked back at Nick. "Meta-what?"

"It means I was exaggerating. They'll explain it in summer school."

"Thanks for reminding me," Dobie said, hurling a stone into the river. I'd been surprised when Dobie had said he wanted to play football in high school. He didn't seem like the type to do an organized sport. Well, not until recently. But I was glad he still wanted to be a part of the team. My parents had told me, after Dobie had come to our house smelling like smoke, with his T-shirt down to his knees, that they would *prefer* it if I spent less time with him. But they were wrong. Dobie still had a good heart even if he now looked tough on the outside. My parents thought Nick was okay because his family went to our church.

Nick went back to his daydream. *"And starting at left tackle,"* he said like he was the announcer introducing himself before a game, *"the freshman . . . Nick Miller."* He finished with a fake cheer.

"You are not going to start as left tackle as a freshman," said Dobie.

"In my dream, I am."

"I just want a spot on JV," I said. "Anything is better than flag football."

"No sport that a girl can play should ever be called football," Dobie said in agreement. "No offense, Caleb. I mean, Tessa is cool, but she wouldn't last a second in a

50

real game. Even though she's got bigger biceps than most of the guys."

"She's pretty fast too," I said, replaying the image of Tessa bolting past the defense like they were standing still.

"That's why she's a runner," Dobie replied.

The funny thing was, Tessa didn't look like a runner. Runners were usually tall and lanky with incredibly long legs. Most people would think she was a soccer player. She had that low center of gravity. She never lost her balance. And Tessa's speed didn't come from stride. It came from horsepower. She just had an engine. Try to tackle her, and all you'd see was a head of long red hair racing by.

I didn't argue with Dobie about girls and football. There was no point arguing about something that would never happen. Besides, I mostly agreed with Dobie. Flag football was not real football. It was a fun way to get ready for try-outs this summer, but it wasn't serious. I knew I'd told Tessa I was in it to win it, but winning the flag football championship game was like winning a fun water-gun fight.

We were on the footbridge over the river when the sun broke through the clouds, lighting up the hillside on the other side of town. I knew Tessa was up there on the trails with Marina and Lexie. It was pretty cool that she could go all out in a football game and then crush a run like it was nothing. She just had a different gear. And she really liked to win. The first time we ever hung out in a public setting, she went insane on the hoop shoot, just lit it up, crushing everyone who challenged her. How could I not like a girl like that?

"Here comes summer," said Nick, squinting into the sunshine.

"So long, winter," I added.

"Goodbye to junior high," said Dobie.

Aaron Parker was at Corner Pizza with Brian Braun. They were playing pool, and there were two girls watching them.

Nick saw them first. "What should we do?" he asked as we walked up to the counter to order our slices.

"Just be cool," Dobie said to us, like we were about to do something embarrassing.

"What does that mean?" Nick asked.

"It means be quiet and don't bother their game," I said.

"I can do that," Nick replied.

We sat down with our pizza and ate in silence. I felt like I was trying to behave in a fancy restaurant. I was afraid to make a weird noise or sip my soda or even move my chair. Not with Aaron, Brian, and two high school girls less than ten yards away. There was too much to lose.

I had just stuffed the last of the crust into my mouth when Aaron came over to our table. He was chalking his cue stick. I thought he was going to ask us to leave, when suddenly a smile spread across his face. "What's up, boys?" he asked, slapping our hands one at a time.

When none of us answered Aaron, Brian jumped in. "You guys play some ball today?" he asked.

"We had a football game," Dobie explained.

"We're on a flag football team," Nick added.

Dobie glared at Nick, then said, "It's no big deal. We don't even take it seriously. I mean, if you can't tackle, what's the point, right?"

"Actually, I learned more about playing quarterback in flag football than I did anywhere else," Brian said. "The game moves fast. You gotta shift around in the pocket, find your receivers quickly. It's no joke."

"For real," Dobie agreed.

"You on the team too?" Aaron asked me.

"Yeah, I play a little of everything. I love QB, though."

"Good man," Brian said approvingly.

"You know Braun's a senior this year," Aaron said, pointing to Brian.

"Think you'll play in college?" I asked, imagining it was what Charlie would ask if he were here.

"Hope so," Brian answered.

"The team's going to need a new QB," Aaron said. "You think you're up for it?"

"Definitely," I said casually. I was doing everything I could do to stay cool. But it wasn't easy. Not when two of the best football players in town were talking to me about being the next quarterback of Pilchuck High School. Maybe jumping off that bridge hadn't been such a dumb idea after all.

They went off to finish their pool game, but before they left the restaurant, Brian stopped as he got to our table. "Hit us up if you want to work out sometime. I've got some passing drills that are pretty good for accuracy. I can walk you through the playbook too."

"Later, fellas," Aaron said to all of us.

When they were gone, Dobie slapped the table. "Boys," he said. "It's official. WE. ARE. IN."

"In what?" Nick asked.

"The circle, the club, the team, whatever," Dobie answered. "Do you know how often varsity football players talk to eighth graders for no reason?" He threw his head back like he was going to howl, then jumped up. "This is so awesome. Caleb, we have to hit them up, soon, but not too soon."

"What about me?" Nick asked.

"Yeah, yeah, all three of us," Dobie corrected himself. "Cool?" he asked me.

"Very cool," I said.

I sprinted home. I couldn't wait to tell Charlie what had happened. He needed to confirm that this was for real— that Aaron and Brian had meant what they said.

There was steak on the grill when I got home. Dad was brushing back smoke and flames as the meat sizzled, while Mom was boiling corn. I smelled biscuits in the oven.

"How long until dinner?" I asked.

Mom gestured to Dad. "Just waiting on the steaks."

I washed my hands and started setting the table. "Where's Charlie?"

"He had something to do," Mom said.

"What?"

"I'm not sure."

"Was he at the shop today?"

The "shop" was the aluminum siding company. My

grandfather had started the business more than fifty years before. Over the years, the company had done the exteriors of half the houses in Pilchuck. Now they had seventeen employees and were still growing quickly. Mom reminded Dad of that whenever he complained about the sprawl that was eating up the open space around our house.

"No," Mom replied. "He hasn't been coming in. Let's not bring it up during dinner."

"Maybe he got a full-time job at the gym," I said.

"I don't think so," Mom answered.

It was a drag that Charlie wasn't home. He was never at the house much, even though he still lived here, but I had hoped he would be this time. I had to get this news off my chest. So I slipped back outside and sent a message to Tessa. My fingers trembled. It was a pretty killer feeling, having news like this to share with someone like her. I was on top of the world.

We sat down for dinner ten minutes later. My brother Luke led grace.

"Tell me about football, Caleb," Dad said.

"We won," I said. "On to the championship game."

"Ooooh," said Luke. "The flag football championship. Do you get cupcakes if you win?"

"Hey, a win's a win," Dad said. "I remember my freshman season. We lost our first ten games. I thought we'd never get one. Finally we ran into a team that was even worse than us, and we beat them. We didn't care who they were. We were just happy to come out on top. Three years later we were playing for the state championship. But you know how that ended."

"Actually, I forgot from the other ten thousand times you've told us," Luke replied.

"They got pounded," I said, smiling at Dad. "But they . . ."

"Held their heads high because they knew they had left it all on the field," Mom, Luke, and I said at the same time.

"You can laugh," Dad said, "but that's a life lesson from a game." He pointed his fork at me and Luke. "You'll both find that out."

"Did you play quarterback today, Caleb?" Mom asked.

"A little bit of everything," I said.

Mom smiled at me from across the table. "Was Tessa there?"

"Well, yeah, she's on the team."

Dad shook his head. "What next?" he asked.

"Actually, she's pretty good," I said. "She caught the winning touchdown."

"Must have been some defense," Dad said.

"We wish we could be at your games," Mom said apologetically. "If it wasn't so busy at work, we'd be there."

"We'll be there in the fall," Dad said. "Fifty-yard line."

"You think they'll build that new stadium?" I asked.

"Not with my money," Dad answered.

"But you love football," Luke said.

"I like my money more."

"Well, congratulations, Caleb," Mom said, bringing the

conversation back to the game. "We're very proud of you. I know you're going to win next week too."

"Thanks," I said. "It's really not a big deal, though. We're just having fun."

I meant it too. I never would have thought the outcome of a flag football game would matter. Boy, was I wrong.

CHAPTER THIRTEEN

→ TESSA

SATURDAY, MAY 21

It was a QB scramble. Caleb was on the move, ducking and dodging tacklers, kicking up dirt and dust, breaking into a full sprint as the clock ticked down to thirty seconds . . . twenty-nine . . . I had done my part, throwing a block that had laid out a linebacker. Now I was watching Caleb weave his way toward the end zone. If he had cut back inside on the ten, he would have scored easily. But for some reason he was running straight down the sideline, and he got his flag pulled from behind—three yards short of the end zone.

We had twenty-eight seconds to move the ball nine feet. We should have been in the huddle, drawing up the next play. But Caleb was celebrating the previous play with Dobie and Nick. It was like they thought we had already won.

"Hey!" I yelled. "We're still *behind*. We haven't scored yet."

Caleb smiled. "Relax, Tessa," he said as we formed a circle. "We got this."

"Not yet," I replied.

Caleb was playing quarterback. Nick was blocking. He used his big body like a wall to protect Caleb while Caleb waited for me or for Dobie to get open. It would have to be a pass. There was no time to run the ball.

"Forty-four eagle on two," Caleb said with a steady voice that made me believe he was sure we were going to win the game. "Don't look back until you're in the end zone."

We clapped and broke the huddle.

Forty-four eagle on two meant that after the snap count, I was supposed to run a slant pattern across the field. It was a timing route. By the time I looked for the ball, it would be in the air, so I had to turn my head at exactly the right moment. We had practiced the play a thousand times. All for this.

I lined up in the slot. When the center snapped the ball, I darted through the defense and broke free as my feet crossed the thick white line in the grass. I was in the end zone with a defender chasing me. He would never catch me now. I whipped my body in the other direction, eyes searching for the ball, hands up at the ready to feel the smack of leather against my palms and the grip of my fingers. There it was, spinning toward me like a big, brown bullet. I was a heartbeat away from being a champion.

And then.

A heartbeat away was long enough for a perfectly thrown ball to bounce off a receiver's hands and into the arms of a safety waiting two yards in front of them. Long enough for a game-winning touchdown to become a game-saving interception. Long enough to smash the dreams of a girl who had had one chance to be a football champion and had blown it. Victory would have been even sweeter than coming in first in the Pilchuck Scramble, because nobody had expected the winning catch to come from a girl. It would have been something special.

I sat by myself after the game. The last play flashed through my mind again and again: the ball spinning toward me before bouncing off my fingertips. My hands had let me down, and I had let my team down. I didn't think I would ever get over it.

Caleb and Nick and Dobie were talking to some of the guys from the other team.

"You won this one," Nick shouted to the defender who had intercepted the final pass. "But we'll get you back this fall. When it counts."

"We'll be ready," the defender called back.

"You better be," Dobie added. "Today was just practice. A warm-up."

"We weren't even playing hard," said Caleb.

Suddenly my grief turned into red-hot anger. Not at myself for letting the ball go off my hands, but at Caleb and Dobie and Nick for acting like this was all a joke. How could Caleb say they hadn't even been playing hard? Was he kidding? What kind of athlete didn't go all out in a championship game—even if it was just flag football? With five words, everything I thought I saw in Caleb disappeared. He wasn't a great competitor with an infectious confidence. He was a clown wasting his own talent—and mine.

Then it got worse.

I watched as a man wearing shorts, a gray shirt, and a green visor walked up to Caleb, Nick, and Dobie. The man smiled and shook the guys' hands one at a time. He handed Caleb a piece of paper before jogging away.

After he left, the three of them danced around like they had just won the lottery. Then Caleb came over to me. Strutting. "Check it out!" he said, handing me the sheet of paper. "Football camp!"

"Who was that?" I asked, holding the piece of paper but not looking at it.

"He's one of the coaches for the high school football team. The, uh, defensive backs coach, or something like that. I can't remember."

"What did he want?"

"He told us we looked good out there and said we should come to a football camp for ninth and tenth graders. It's in July. He said it's like a warm-up for tryouts. Awesome, right?"

"Did he say anything about me?" I didn't know what I expected. There was no reason a high school football coach would be interested in me. My entire gender was ineligible for high school football, and I had just dropped the game-winning pass. Maybe I just wanted to punish Caleb with an awkward moment.

"U-um, no," Caleb stuttered. "He didn't. But I could ask him if girls can go. Or maybe there's a . . ."

Caleb stopped midsentence.

"You say cheerleading camp, you die."

"You're not a cheerleader," he said. "You're a wide receiver."

"Not anymore," I replied.

There was no better way to explain it to Caleb. Losing one flag football game was not the end of the world. And maybe if we had gotten blown out, I wouldn't have been so upset. But that wasn't what had happened. I would forever be stuck with the image of those final seconds of the last football game I would ever play, unable to ever make up for it.

Now every time I thought about the play, I couldn't help wondering about football camp. I read more online. The first thing I saw was that all the pictures were of boys. That wasn't surprising. But I also noticed that the rules didn't say anything about girls. I clicked on a link labeled eligibility. It said you had to be entering ninth or tenth grade, live in Pilchuck, and have permission from a legal guardian. That was all. I went back to Google, typed *girls playing football,* and learned there were more than sixteen hundred girls playing high school football across the country, and some of them lived not too far from me. Also, there were more injuries in cheerleading than in football.

I closed my laptop with a mixture of nerves and excitement. Knowing that nobody (except my legal guardians) could stop me from signing up for football camp was a bit thrilling and also a bit crazy-scary at the same time. If I wanted to be a football player, I had to take the next step. Assuming I could convince my parents. All I needed to do was figure out how this would make me the successful daughter they had always wanted.

CHAPTER FOURTEEN

→ CALEB

Tessa took the loss pretty hard. Too hard, if you ask me. It was just a game, even if it was the last one she would ever play. I figured Tessa was mostly mad at herself for not catching that pass. The thing was that while none of the rest of us liked losing either, we didn't care that much. We knew the score, but to us it was really about getting ready for fall football.

Later that night I started to text her just to see how she was doing.

"Don't do it," said Charlie, passing by me on his way to the refrigerator.

Charlie was dressed in track pants and a golf shirt from the Pilchuck Athletic Club, where he worked part-time as a personal trainer. If I wanted to get in shape lifting weights, I would listen to Charlie. Dude was ripped. He knew it too. I also listened to Charlie when it came to girls.

"Don't do what?" I asked. "You don't even know what I'm doing."

"You're sending a text to someone who wants to be left alone."

"I just want to ask her if she's feeling better." I was looking down at the half-written message on my phone, when it suddenly buzzed in my hands. It was a message from Charlie—sent from across the room.

It said, *She isn't.*

I turned around to see Charlie shaking his head. "Delete it. Trust me."

"What's the big deal?" I asked.

"You know how it is, man," he said. "Doesn't matter if it's death or sports, you don't mess with someone when they're grieving. Your job is to shut up and stay away. When she's over it, you'll hear from her. But you have to let her grieve."

"Really?" I asked.

Charlie nodded. "Really. Let her grieve."

"Who's grieving?" asked Luke, walking into the kitchen wearing pajama bottoms, headphones, and no shirt. He found a bag of ham in the refrigerator and began dangling slices into his mouth.

"You are," said Charlie.

"Why am I grieving?" Luke asked.

"Because you have a giant bruise on your arm."

Luke stopped inhaling ham long enough to glance at his arm. He barely had time to say "No, I don't" before Charlie popped him right where he'd been looking. "Gaaa!" Luke wailed. "That did NOT hurt."

"Hey, are we still camping next weekend?" I asked.

"Absolutely," said Charlie. "Dad's driving us to the trail-head, and we're hiking up to Bear Lake. Two-thousand-feet gain in four miles." Charlie held his hand at a steep angle. "You guys better be ready."

"I'm not carrying the bricks again," said Luke. "I don't get why we even bring bricks on a hike."

"To keep the tent from blowing away," said Charlie, like it was obvious.

"Can't we just use stakes?" Luke asked. "Or rocks?"

"Bricks are better," I said. "Besides, it's a family tradition."

"Tradition is important," Charlie added.

Luke left the kitchen mumbling about the unfairness of it all. When he was out of the room, Charlie and I cracked up. We'd both had to carry the bricks. We hadn't been lying about it being a family tradition, but it had nothing to do with the tent. It was just mean. Funny mean, but mean.

CHAPTER FIFTEEN

↳TESSA

FRIDAY, MAY 27

The end of the game invaded my brain. It took control of my mind. During study hall on Tuesday, I read a chapter about World War I. When I got to the end, the only thing I could recall was the memory of losing by three points. On Wednesday, I lay awake trying to think about anything else. I listed my friends in alphabetical order, counted the states I had been to, and played a game of Scrabble in my head. (I lost.) I went for a run on Thursday, and even that didn't help. I actually made up words to the beat of my feet hitting the ground. *You. Lost. The. Game. That's it. For life.*

At school on Friday, football wasn't exactly a hot topic at the girls' lunch table. Lexie and Marina were into sports, like me, but they weren't very sympathetic or actually really interested in spending time discussing it. They didn't even pick up on the fact that something was wrong, until I sighed sadly.

"Something wrong? Are you and Caleb in a fight?" Marina asked, barely looking up from her chemistry textbook. She was studying for her final exam.

"I can't stop thinking about the game," I said, relieved to say it out loud.

"What game?" Lexie asked.

"Our last flag football game," I replied. "We were so close to winning. It's killing me. I would do anything for another chance."

"Well, that's not going to happen," Marina said. "I mean, unless you found a way to play football again. And wasn't that just something you did for fun on a few Saturdays? Not like a real legit thing, was it?"

"I'm not even sure anymore," I mumbled. The loss had really messed with my head. I was completely revealing how much I enjoyed playing flag football with the boys, something I never talked about in front of my best friends. I barely told them I played at all. "I'm never playing with those boys again. Did I tell you what happened after the game?"

"I'm guessing something gross, illegal, or both," Marina replied. "I mean, except for your boyfriend, Mr. Perfect." She smiled devilishly.

"I never said he was perfect."

"Well, then what did he do?" Lexie asked.

"A coach from the high school football team asked them to go to some stupid football camp this summer."

Lexie and Marina barely reacted.

"Is that bad?" Lexie asked.

"Yes!" I said. "Now their egos are even bigger. But the worst part is, they weren't even mad about losing. They were laughing and talking about how life goes on, which I guess it does. But now Caleb, who is supposed to, you know, care what I think, is totally ignoring me." I didn't go into any details about what that meant, since you could technically have said I was ignoring him too.

"Kind of sounds like this isn't really about football, Tessa," Marina said.

"Then what is it about?" I asked.

"I think you just want someone to feel sorry for you," Lexie said.

Deep down, I knew they were right. I hated the way the game had ended, and I was jealous that the boys would get to play football again. But what really bothered me was that nobody seemed to understand my pain.

"Anyway," said Marina, "enough about football. In case you forgot, we are runners. With bright futures."

"Destined for greatness," Lexie added.

"We'll make varsity for sure," said Marina, finally closing the chemistry book. "Half of the cross-country team last year was seniors. Am I right, Tess?"

"Tess?" Lexie asked. "You with us?"

"All the way," I said. "Fast and furious."

Marina and Lexie continued to talk at warp speed about how the three of us were going to rock the cross-country team together. We would steal the show from the football team and become overnight legends. We'd be three champions winning state, ribbons hanging from our necks and trophies in our hands. All courage and speed and heart. Three *amigas*.

Deep down, I really wanted to mean it. As my best friends kept talking, I truly wanted to run cross-country with them, but a part of me also wanted to play football with the boys. I was kidding myself to think both things were possible. They weren't. I realized I was going to have to choose between what everyone expected me to do and what I in my heart wanted to do. This thought was something completely new. What if I didn't do what was expected of me? What if I played football? Was that something I really wanted? Or was it something I wanted because everyone didn't think I would do it?

When I got home from school, Mom and Dad were at the dining room table in plain view of the front door. In the front hall was a stack of campaign signs, the kind that people put in their front yards. All the signs said the same thing: JANE DOOLEY FOR MAYOR.

Mom was pecking on her laptop, muttering to herself. Dad was on his phone, holding it a few inches from his face with his mouth open, like he thought it would never be his turn to speak. Still, from the way his eyes lit up whenever he was able to talk about why Mom was running, I could see he was enjoying the campaign. Ever since he had quit his job fixing computers at an insurance company so he could help Mom work in the political sphere, there'd been a new sparkle in his eyes. I wished he'd have any kind of sparkle when I told him news about school, or my friends, or sports.

"Hi," I said. "I'm home. School was okay, thanks for asking." I dropped my keys onto the counter and looked over at them. Now Dad was typing and Mom was on her phone. "There was an earthquake today," I said casually. "The school was destroyed. I was the only survivor. Aren't you happy to see me?"

No answer.

My family was not interested in my problems either.

"Tessa, is that you?" Mom asked.

"No, it's just a burglar with keys to your house," I said. "Please keep doing whatever you're doing while I rob you."

"Thanks, sweetie," Mom answered. "We'll be done soon."

"We're setting up interviews for next week," Dad explained. "Your mom's going to be on the news," he added.

"You mean like that dog that rides a skateboard?" I asked.

"Yup," said Dad. But not to me. It was finally his turn to speak on the phone. "Still here."

I laced up my running shoes a few minutes later, grabbed an energy bar from the cabinet, and headed for the door. Before I left the house, I looked at my phone one more time. No messages.

And then someone knocked.

CHAPTER SIXTEEN
→ CALEB

On Friday, I made plans with Nick and Dobie to play two-on-one football in Boardman Park after school. But I had another mission to accomplish first. I was going to stop by Tessa's house. I had to see her. I needed to know that she wasn't mad at me. It had been a week since I'd talked to her, and I couldn't stand the idea of anyone being mad at me. Especially her.

When the school bell rang, I darted for the door.

But Nick and Dobie caught up to me.

"Caleb, wait up," Nick called. "You heading to the park? We'll walk with you."

The hallway was filling up with people pushing and jostling their way toward the exit. Dobie and I stood flat against the lockers, but Nick had nowhere to hide.

"I'll meet you at the park," I told Nick and Dobie. "I have something to do."

"What?" Nick asked.

"Just something," I answered.

Dobie glanced at Nick, who exhaled dramatically.

"You guys have a problem?"

"Why don't you just admit you're ditching us for your girlfriend?" Dobie asked.

"And don't pretend she's just a friend," Nick added, putting *friend* in air quotes. "We know the truth. Roy saw you guys holding hands outside of Pilchuck Market."

"All right," I said. "I guess, yeah, it's more than friends. I don't know exactly what you call it, though."

"Just say it," Dobie demanded. "Say what she is."

"You already know," I told him.

"We want to hear it," Nick answered.

"Fine. If it'll shut you up. Tessa is my girlfriend."

"Congratulations," Dobie said sarcastically. "I hope you two are very happy together."

"Thank you," I said. "Can I go now?"

"Okay," said Nick. "But make it quick. You turned in your permission slip, right?" he asked.

"For football camp? Yeah. We're good. I'm in."

I jogged all the way to Tessa's street. When I could see her house, I slowed down until I was sure I wasn't breathing hard. If her parents were home, I didn't want to look like some crazy guy who had run all over town chasing their daughter. Plus, I had to think about what I was going to say. My gut told me to say I was sorry, but then I realized I didn't know what I was sorry for. Telling her I missed her, which was true, sounded like something I would say to my grandmother. In the end, I decided to go with whatever came out of my mouth.

Tessa's house was half brick and half wood. It was set back from the street and partially hidden by two big oak trees that shaded the whole front yard, where her dog, Oreo, was currently sleeping with one eye open. Oreo blinked at me, then rolled onto his back. After stopping to scratch his chest, I walked up to the door. I blew on my hands for good luck and knocked.

A minute later, I was looking at Tessa.

"Hi," she said.

She had on her yellow running shorts and a blue tank top. Her hair was pulled back into a ponytail like it always was when she was going for a run. Anyone could have easily seen that that was what she planned to do next.

"Um, going for a run?" I asked.

Tessa nodded. "With Marina and Lexie. In Boardman Park."

"That's where I'm going," I said.

"But you came here," Tessa pointed out.

"Well, I mean, that's where I'm going next. I came to your house first."

"That's nice," Tessa replied.

We didn't say anything for a minute. Over on the grass, Oreo rolled over with a snort. We both looked at him.

"Well," Tessa said. "I gotta run."

"Are you mad at me?" I finally asked.

CHAPTER SEVENTEEN
→ TESSA

Caleb seemed so confused. He obviously knew something was wrong but had no idea what it was. There was suffering in his brown eyes, and I had the power to make it go away. It was the right thing to do. I hoped if I was ever in his position, someone would do the same for me. So I told him the truth.

"I was mad at you because you weren't mad at me," I said.

"Why would I be mad at you?" Caleb asked, inching closer. "Because of the way the game ended? I don't care about that."

I gave him a little shove. "That's what I mean. I wanted you to care."

"No, I mean, I care about the game," Caleb replied, waving his hands. "I totally wanted to win. But I would never be mad at you for not making a catch. Seriously, that was a tough play, and I figured if you couldn't do it, nobody could."

"You mean that?"

"You're a good football player, and I'm not just saying you're good for a girl. If I was picking teams . . ."

"You'd pick me first?"

Caleb smiled. "Well, I can't say first for sure. But top five definitely."

Wow. This guy knew the way to my heart. "Really?"

Caleb nodded. "Yeah, you're fast. You've got good hands. You run tight routes. And you want to win as bad as anyone else I know."

"I wish I had caught that ball," I replied.

"I wish you could go to football camp so you'd have a redo. I think that's the only thing that would help me."

My heart did a little end-zone dance. "Thank you."

There wasn't much more to say about football, so we made plans to walk up to the ridge after my run with the girls.

The ridge was a steep half-mile hike to a spot with a view of the whole town. As we cruised up the trail, Caleb seemed on top of the world about everything. He was "beyond pumped" about going camping with his brothers, even though they wouldn't be able to fish. He was "losing his mind" about seeing *Octosaur,* and he asked me if I'd go with him. And he was "on fire" about football tryouts in the fall.

I wasn't jealous about camping, and I didn't really want to see *Octosaur,* but when he mentioned football camp, I bit my lip with envy.

"I know it's still more than a month away," he said, "but

me and Nick and Dobie are going to start training as soon as school's over. Charlie said he'd set us up with weights and a bench in the garage, and we'll run the stairs in the grandstand."

"Sounds fun," I said as we came within a hundred yards of the ridge.

"Oh, it's going to be brutal," Caleb replied. "You'd love it."

I was probably reading too much into it, but in that moment, what I heard Caleb say was *You should do it too.* Could you blame me, after everything he had actually said? His belief in me as a player was giving me ideas, crazy ideas, and before I knew it, there were fireworks going off in my mind. And it was all because of Caleb, who understood me and gave me that extra confidence I needed to keep playing.

Lots of people had climbed to the ridge to watch the sunset. We found a flat rock to sit on and leaned back, side by side, against the trunk of an alder tree.

"Do you really think I could play football?" I asked.

"Definitely."

"What if I'm not fast enough?"

"You are."

"What if I don't know where to run?"

"You will."

"What if my hands are too small?"

"Let me see," Caleb said.

I held out my hands.

"Hold one up," he said.

I lifted my left hand, and Caleb pressed his palm against

mine. His top knuckles met my fingertips. "See. I have small hands."

Before Caleb could answer, there was a flash of light, and a man with a badge hanging around his neck was looking at his camera.

"Great shot," he said to himself. Then he looked up at us. "You two want to be in the paper?" he asked.

Chapter Eighteen
→ CALEB

SATURDAY, MAY 28

Charlie and Luke destroyed me when they saw the picture in the paper. It was right there on the front page, Tessa and me, our hands locked together as the sun set behind us. The caption read: *Summer love on the ridge as Tessa Dooley and Caleb McCleary, both 14, enjoy the sunset over Pilchuck.* Charlie harassed me during the whole drive up to the trailhead.

By the time Dad put the truck in park, I was ready to leave civilization behind. I swore I would never let anyone print my name in the paper again. We strapped on our packs in the gravel parking lot. The sun had burned through the last of the morning clouds. It was going to be hot and dry. Charlie had already taken off his T-shirt.

Luke and I grabbed our fishing poles from the bed of the truck.

"No fishing," Dad said.

"Nobody's going to know," Luke protested.

"Rangers patrol the lakes, Luke. Season doesn't open for another week," Dad said. "They catch you, you're going to get fined, which means I'm going to have to pay. So, no fishing."

Charlie walked over holding his pole. "We're just going to practice casting," he said. "We don't even have bait."

"Just casting," Dad repeated.

"Scout's honor," Charlie said.

"I hope I can count on you for this at least," Dad told Charlie, before driving off in the truck.

Charlie watched Dad disappear down the mountain. "Screw it," he said. "Let's go fishing."

Luke and I followed Charlie single file up the trail. We moved quickly, stopping only twice for water. After two hours of hard hiking, we arrived at the lake and set up camp on an outcrop shaded by the small mountain peak behind us. A light breeze blew cool air off the last of the snowpack.

"What are we going to do now?" Luke asked.

"We're gonna fish," said Charlie, like it was a stupid question.

"You mean cast?" I asked.

"Nooo," said Charlie, digging a jar of bait out of his pack. "I mean fish. Luke was right for once in his life. Nobody's gonna know. We're the only ones here."

"Dad said not to," Luke grumbled.

"Is Dad always right?" Charlie asked angrily.

"No," Luke admitted.

"Then shut up and fish," Charlie shot back.

Luke and I baited our hooks and followed Charlie to the lake. Pretty soon we were all standing in the water casting and waiting for the fish to bite.

Luke rubbed his stomach. "I'm hungry. What's for dinner?"

For a long time, the only sounds we heard were the whine of our lines unreeling and mosquitoes buzzing in the warm air. We fished for more than an hour, but none of us caught anything big enough to keep. I think defying Dad made Charlie feel better, because he was in a happier mood as dusk fell. We made a small fire outside our tents and roasted hot dogs. After we ate, Luke put on a headlamp and propped himself against a tree to read, leaving Charlie and me to watch the fire.

I hoped Charlie would ask about Tessa. I wanted him to tell me everything he knew about having a girlfriend. I needed information, and he was the only one who could help me. Nick and Dobie had never had girlfriends, and I had questions I would never ask Dad. I stayed quiet for as long as I could, thinking Charlie might start the conversation, because I didn't know where to begin. But he just stared into the flames, poking the coals with a long stick.

"I'm not going to change my mind," he said finally.

"About what?" I asked.

Charlie looked straight ahead, like he was talking to the fire. "I'm not going to work at the shop. I'm not going to spend my life installing aluminum siding. I'm going to be a physical therapist. I don't care what Dad says or does."

"Maybe you could just work there for a couple of years and then be a physical therapist," I said.

"No," Charlie replied, shaking his head. "If I do that, I'll never leave."

"Leave where?" I asked.

Charlie didn't answer.

The wind shifted, blowing smoke into my eyes. I moved to the opposite side of the fire pit. "Leave where?" I repeated.

"Hey," Charlie replied a moment later. "So you've got a girlfriend?"

"Yeah," I said. "I guess I do."

"That's a good thing, man. You know what you're doing?"

"What am I doing?"

"No," Charlie corrected me. "I mean, do you have this under control?"

"Not really," I admitted. "All I know is, a few weeks ago she wasn't my girlfriend and now she is, and I can't really tell what's different."

"The difference is, she comes first now."

"First before what?"

"Before anything," Charlie explained. "She goes through the door first. You call her before you call your friends. You don't eat until she eats. You don't speak until she speaks."

"You're kidding, right?"

Charlie laughed. "Only kind of," he said. "Look, what I think is that you can't let one girl change your life too much. You have to keep being you. You gotta have your friends. Other than that, just make sure to have fun. You're not ready for anything more than that."

"Are there rules?" I asked.

"Oh, you want to know the rules?" Charlie asked. "I've got 'em written down here. Everything you need to know." He reached into his pocket and pulled out a crumpled piece of paper. "You want it? This is sacred. Dad gave it to me when I was your age. I carry it with me everywhere."

"Definitely," I said. I couldn't believe it. Charlie was giving me the playbook for having a girlfriend!

Charlie tossed the paper onto the fire. "Too bad," he said.

"Why did you do that?" I asked, horrified.

"It was a grocery receipt, stupid," Charlie said. "There are no rules. Just be yourself and make her happy."

"You're a punk," I said.

"Takes one to know one, Romeo." Charlie stood up. "I'm going to find a tree."

I felt like a dope for thinking Charlie had really had a list of rules. But mostly I was relieved. Knowing there weren't rules was as good as knowing there were rules. Maybe even better. Be myself and make Tessa happy. What could be hard about that?

Not far off, I saw the light from Luke's headlamp darting around inside his tent. A moment later, he was walking over to the fire. There was a brick in his hand. "It's a joke, isn't it?" he asked. "You guys made me carry these for no reason."

"You'll have to ask Charlie," I responded.

"I hate him," Luke said, finding a spot beside me.

"You'd miss him if he were gone," I said.

CHAPTER NINETEEN
→TESSA

SUNDAY, MAY 29

Everyone had an opinion about the photo in the paper. Caleb and I had told the photographer he could use it because we thought it would be cool. Now I wasn't so sure. Lexie said it was real. Marina said it was cinematic. Dad said I was too young to be in a couple. I didn't know what Caleb thought, because he'd left early Saturday morning to camp with his brothers.

There was no question what Mom thought, though.

"Why is this front-page news?" she asked, like it had been up to me. Mom was sitting on the couch with a reporter while a cameraman set up lights. She was about to be interviewed for the local news. Mom had won the primary the week before, which was like a semifinal for politicians. It meant she would be one of two candidates that people could vote for in the November election.

"It's not like the sun sets every day," I said, obviously joking.

"It's a human-interest story, Jane," Dad explained to Mom. "It has visual appeal. It sells papers." He sat on the edge of the coffee table facing the couch, where Mom and I were sitting. "Let's focus on the interview."

"Three minutes, Jane," said the reporter.

"Sounds good," Mom said.

"She's going to ask you about three things," Dad said. "She'll ask about your record on the city council. She'll ask you about your opponent. And she'll ask about school funding and the stadium."

I knew what Dad meant about the last thing. The school district didn't have enough money to pay the teachers and fix the schools, so some of the people on the city council wanted to raise taxes. Like she'd said before, Mom thought the school district should save money by cutting "nonessential" projects, like a new football stadium. This was going to be an issue with a lot of people in Pilchuck.

"One minute," said the reporter.

"We need the daughter out of the shot," the cameraman said.

I stood up, but the reporter gestured for me to sit. "No," she said. "Let's keep her. You don't mind, right?" she asked, looking at Mom.

Before Mom could answer, the cameraman had snapped a tiny microphone to my shirt.

"Councilwoman?" said Beth to my mother. "Is it okay if

we interview your daughter on the air? I'd love for the voters to meet a member of your wonderful family."

Mom strained to put on a smile. "Well, sure!"

This was the first time she had ever needed to share the spotlight, to acknowledge my presence for more than five minutes. This would be good.

She forcefully laid her notes on her lap. It was the last time she looked at them. Because the reporter didn't ask any questions about taxes or schools or parks.

"We're here in the living room of City Councilwoman Jane Dooley, who recently won her party's primary. How are you feeling about the upcoming general election?" Beth asked.

Mom smiled back at the camera. "I am looking forward to an open and positive discussion about the issues that matter to all of us living in Pilchuck." Mom paused and extended her pointer finger, which I knew meant she wanted to list the reasons she was running for mayor. But she didn't get a chance.

"Wonderful," Beth replied, cutting her off. "And who do you have with you?"

"This is my heart and joy, my daughter, Tessa."

"Tessa, you're becoming quite a media star," Beth said. "First you get your picture on the front page of the *Pilchuck Observer*, and now a televised interview. Can you tell me who was with you in the photo?"

"A friend. My friend. Caleb."

"Just a friend? Or boyfriend?"

"Just a friend," Mom cut in and answered.

"So what do you like to do, Tessa?"

"She's a wonderful runner," Mom interrupted. "Cross-country. She's very fast."

It was something about the way she said it. Like she knew exactly what I did and what I liked. Like she listened and noticed. Which she didn't.

"I also play football," I spurted.

Beth looked surprised. "You mean soccer?"

"No," I said. "I mean football. I played flag football this spring. And I'm going to go to football camp this summer. It's like a warm-up for tryouts," I added. I knew I was lighting a fuse, but I had to take control. I couldn't let Mom tell me and the whole world what mattered in my life. I was finally ready to break their expectations.

"You're what?" Mom asked.

Beth looked back and forth from me to Mom. "Oh, looks like we have some breaking news here in the Dooley household."

Lesson learned. Once you say something on TV, you can't really take it back.

"How much trouble am I in?" I asked Dad after the news crew had left and Mom had gone for a run.

"It depends," Dad answered.

"On what?" I asked.

"On whether we can spin this," he said, anxiously scrolling on his phone. "It was definitely not the interview we wanted, but we might get lucky if people identify with your mom as a mother with an unpredictable but appealing family. We can use that as a stepping-stone to talking about the real issues."

"Dad, what are you talking about?"

"Huh?"

"I didn't understand anything you just said."

"You don't have to, sweetie. It's just politics. We'll take care of it. Just need a little damage control."

"What about the other thing?" I asked.

"What other thing?"

"The football thing," I said.

"That's a tough call," Dad replied. "It could play out a couple of ways. Voters might respond positively if they see it as a just cause—or it could backfire if they think we're pushing the envelope on equality."

"Yeah, but what do you think about me playing football? Do you think I'd be good? Can I do it?"

"I don't know," Dad said. "I've never seen you play."

A moment later, Dad's phone rang and I left the room, wondering if anything would ever change.

CHAPTER TWENTY
→ CALEB

Dad picked us up on Sunday afternoon. We tossed our gear into the back of the truck and headed home. I didn't know it yet, but by then, Tessa had been on TV and all over the media.

It was Charlie who saw it first.

"Holy . . . ," he said from the passenger seat.

"What?" I asked.

He passed his phone back to me.

The headline on the screen read, PILCHUCK TEEN, 14, DECLARES FOOTBALL AMBITIONS, UPSTAGING MOM. I clicked on the link and skimmed the article, not really believing that it was about Tessa. I told myself it had to be about some other Tessa with the same last name whose mom was also running for mayor, because that made more sense than a girl going to football camp. I knew I had told Tessa she could play football, but that didn't mean I thought she *should*. First, football was a guys' sport. Second, I did not want to look over in the huddle and see my girlfriend starting at me through a face mask.

"What do I do?" I said.

"Simple," Charlie answered. "Make it go away."

"What do you mean? Just tell her she can't play?"

"There's no question she can't play," Charlie said. "What I'm saying is that you can't let her even think about it."

"You think anyone else knows yet?"

"Have you checked your phone?"

"No."

"Might want to look."

I opened my phone. Thirteen new texts. Dobie, Nick, Julian, Ruben, Khalil, and a bunch of numbers I didn't even know. Plus two from Tessa.

Dude, seriously? Is this a joke?

BWAA HA HA HA!

My mom is sooo mad.

Did we trade you to the cheerleaders?

I hope they make punk shoulder pads.

Puke.

PINK! I meant pink shoulder pads. I hate my phone.

U there?

She knows it's TACKLE football, right?

This CANNOT happen.

If a girl can play on the football team, does that

mean my dog can run track? Cause she's crazy fast.

I mean my dog.

McCleary, Coach says no holding hands in the huddle.
Call me when you can.

The third and the last ones were from Tessa.

After stopping at home to shower and change, I ran down to Pilchuck Market to meet Tessa. She was sitting on a bench in front of the store wearing light blue track pants, a white tank top, and a green visor. She waved when she saw me.

"Hi," she said.

"Hey," I said back, wondering who was going to say it first.

We went inside to buy food. Tessa bought a bottle of water and a granola bar. I got a hot dog and a soda. The clerk at the counter smiled at Tessa. "The football girl," he said.

"That's me," she replied. She turned to me, beaming. "I'm famous."

"Yeah, I heard." I paid for our food and followed Tessa back to the bench. "So, you really want to play football?" I asked.

"You know I do," she answered.

I took a bite of my hot dog. "I do?"

"We talked about it, like, two days ago."

"Well, yeah, but I didn't think . . ."

Tessa unscrewed the cap from her water bottle. "What?"

"I mean, I didn't know you *really* wanted to play."

"Oh God, now you sound like my mom."

I stopped chewing and wondered if this was the most

uncomfortable moment of my life. I thought about walking out of town and never coming back.

"Why would I say I did if I didn't mean it?" Tessa asked after a long sip.

"Because it's, you know," I said, trying not to dig myself into a deeper hole.

"Yeah?"

I was going to say *because football isn't for girls,* but I held up, like a batter checking his swing. Tessa was so revved up about this. How could I talk her out of playing football when I had already told her she was good at it? On the other hand, if I ignored my friends, they'd ice me out. I couldn't live with that. "It's a rough sport," I said at last.

"I can handle it," Tessa answered. "Can you?"

"Hey, I'm a freak of nature," I said, flexing my arms. "Look at these guns."

Tessa barely laughed. "I don't even know if I'm allowed to play," she said. "There might be rules against it."

"Hey, rules are made to be broken, right?"

"Wait," Tessa said, looking perplexed. "You just told me it was a rough sport. Now you're saying I should go for it?"

"Well, I wasn't saying that exactly."

"What were you saying?"

"What do you mean?"

"It just sounds like you want it both ways, Caleb."

"Who cares what I want?" I said, trying to be breezy.

"Sooner or later you're going to have to pick a side."

We ended the football conversation. Tessa went to meet her friends. I went home. As I walked, I thought about picking sides. The whole thing was confusing. Part of me was into the idea of Tessa trying out for the football team, even though it was crazy and she'd never make it. But if I was being honest, I really wished the whole thing would just go away.

CHAPTER TWENTY-ONE

→TESSA

At the edge of Boardman Park, where the fields met the woods, there was a spot where Marina, Lexie, and I always cooled down after a run. I loved the view of the grandstand and the mountains behind it.

"Wow," said Lexie, looking at her phone. "We made awesome time."

"There's no way we're not making the cross-country team," Marina said.

I saw Lexie look sideways at Marina. "What?" I asked.

"What do you mean, what?" Lexie responded.

"Something's going on," I said. "I can tell."

"Well, we were just wondering," Marina started.

"Wondering what?

Lexie finished the sentence. "How you plan to play two sports at once."

"Oh, that," I said. Obviously Marina and Lexie had seen the news, but we hadn't actually *had the talk* about what it meant. In my head I knew I had to choose between cross-country and football. I just hadn't admitted it to myself yet. Or the fact that I wanted to play football more than running cross-country.

"Yeah," Marina replied. "That."

"Well, you know I love running with you guys."

"But?"

"But I also love football. And I think I'm pretty good at it. Or I could be. Plus, I feel like I've got this thing hanging over me, and if I don't do something about it, it's going to bug me forever. Also, I don't want to spend the rest of my life helping my mom run for Congress."

"I think you lost me," Marina answered. "Did you say *Congress*? Aren't we just talking about running? Because on top of this, you never told us your mother was running for mayor either. You don't tell us anything anymore."

"I'm sorry. I was trying to block that from my mind," I said. "Don't you guys ever get frustrated with other people making decisions for you? Like you're in a play reading lines someone else wrote and you just want to say what's in your head and not what's on the page?"

"Are you talking about us?" Lexie asked. "Because you're free to make your own decisions, Tessa. And it kind of sounds like you already have."

"I haven't decided anything. I'm just not sure what I want to do right now. I'm not even sure I'm allowed to play football."

"Well," Lexie replied, "maybe after you figure it out, you can go on the news and tell us."

"Are you guys leaving?" I asked.

"Sorry," Marina said. "Gotta run."

I watched as my two best friends left me. I had never felt lonelier. I had always thought they would be there no matter what I did. A scary thought crept into my mind. What would happen now if football didn't work out? I could get hurt or not make the team or not even be allowed to play. Would my best friends take me back?

Chapter Twenty-Two

→ CALEB

FRIDAY, JUNE 3

"Eight—one thousand. Nine—one thousand . . . Ten!" I relaxed my upper body and let the bar rest on the metal arms with a slight clang. I sat up on the bench and pumped my fist, exhaling heavily. "Yeah, baby!" I had just pressed 180 pounds ten times. I felt like the Incredible Hulk.

"Not bad," said Charlie, who had been spotting me. It was a week before the end of school, and we were in the garage. The door was open, letting in the warm breeze. Country music played on the radio. Luke was there too, going a few rounds with the heavy bag Dad had hung from the ceiling.

"Not bad?" I said. "Look at me. I'm ripped."

"You're not ripped," Charlie said. "When you get into the locker room, you'll see ripped."

Luke wound up and gave the canvas one last round-house. Then he roared.

"What's wrong with you?" Charlie asked.

"I punished that bag!"

We watched him beat his chest.

"Man, not you too," said Charlie. "What do you guys think? Lifting weights and punching a bag makes you superheroes?"

"I wouldn't want to fight me," said Luke.

"Both of you, just relax," Charlie said. "You want to work out to get stronger for sports or whatever? That's awesome. But don't make this about girls or brawling."

"Why not?" Luke asked.

Charlie added two twenty-pound discs to the bar I had been lifting. "Because it won't work and you'll just be a bigger version of the dumb punk you already are. Now spot me."

Halfway through Charlie's reps, a shadow appeared on the concrete floor of the garage. I looked over and saw Dad standing in the doorway. The glow of the streetlight made his gray hair look white.

"Hey, Dad," I said. "You want to do a few reps?"

Dad smiled and pointed to his back. "I don't think I have it in me," he said. "Doctor's orders. And your mom's."

"Maybe you should try yoga," Luke suggested. "It's supposed to be good for your back."

"I'd rather join a knitting club," Dad answered. He looked at me. "I need you at the shop tomorrow."

"Yeah, sure," I said.

"What about me?" Luke asked.

"Not till you're fourteen," Dad answered with a sigh. "It's the law."

We were all quiet for a minute while Dad began looking absentmindedly through a box on a shelf.

Charlie broke the silence. "Dad, you know I'd be there, but I have to work all week. Towels aren't going to wash themselves."

"You do what you have to do, Charlie," Dad said.

Before Charlie could respond, another figure appeared in the doorway. It was Tessa, in a pair of gym shorts and a gray hoodie. I prayed she had come to tell me she'd changed her mind about football camp.

"Hi," she said.

"Hey, it's the football girl," said Luke.

I jumped up and jogged over to her and my dad.

"I watched your mom on TV," Dad said.

"Thanks," Tessa replied.

"I'll see you tomorrow," Dad reminded me before going into the house.

"You want to come in?" I asked Tessa when Dad was gone. I hoped she noticed my arms.

Tessa pointed at the bag. "Can I do that?"

Luke tossed her the gloves. "They're sweaty."

"If she had a problem with sweaty hands, she wouldn't be hanging around with this guy," Charlie said, gesturing at me.

"Shut up," I said to Charlie, knowing I might pay for it later.

Tessa blushed but she took off her sweatshirt and put on the gloves. "So I just hit it?" she asked, tapping one glove against the bag.

"Spread your feet apart a bit," I said, standing next to her now. "And put your right foot slightly forward." I pointed to a spot on the concrete floor. Tessa slid her foot toward the bag. "Yeah, like that," I said. "Now drop your left arm a little and punch with your right."

Tessa's first few punches were weak. The bag hardly moved.

"Come on!" Charlie barked. "You hit like a light breeze. Punch like a man!" That was his way of encouraging her. And it worked.

Tessa went after the bag like it had slapped her in the hallway. She landed three or four solid punches before trying a jab with her left. Now the bag was rocking back and forth on the chain and Tessa was hopping from side to side to stay in front of it. That was when I noticed her arms. Not muscular. I doubted she could bench-press thirty pounds. But they were cut; solid lean muscle. I was impressed and a little afraid.

Chapter Twenty-Three

→ TESSA

Caleb handed me a Gatorade and took one for himself. "Green okay?"

"As long as it's cold," I said, hoping he would say right away that he'd been wrong and that I should definitely go to football camp.

We brought our drinks to the backyard and sat on the edge of the empty hot tub, dangling our bare feet in the warm air. I took a sip of Gatorade and exhaled the last of the anger. It had been a week since Lexie and Marina had called me a liar, but it still hurt. Something about the punching bag had brought the anger out. I knew in my heart what they'd said wasn't true. I had changed my mind and had neglected to tell them. About football. About my mom. That was different from lying, and it was my right. If one of them had told me they wanted to try something besides running, I would have been cool with it. My life. My choice. Not theirs.

"I saw your mom on the news," Caleb said. "She was talking about you."

"That's because the more she talks about me, the more she gets on TV."

"I thought you liked being famous."

"She's using me," I said. "And she's a hypocrite. She's telling everyone she's proud of me for doing something that she never really knew about or paid attention to before. She hasn't ever noticed anything I've done. As long as I don't mess up, I don't exist. It's just her and her job. Even my dad is wrapped up in her career. That's why I said what I did on TV. Because I wanted her to hear me say that what I do is up to me, not her anymore."

"Because you want to play football?"

"Because in our house, she's the only story."

"Maybe football isn't dramatic enough," Caleb said. "What if you took up bobsledding? Imagine how big a story that would be if you made the Olympics."

"Bobsledding?" I asked. "Are you serious?" I looked at Caleb. I liked being around him and didn't want to risk losing him now. But he was really starting to let me down.

"It was just an idea," he said awkwardly.

I twisted the cap back onto the Gatorade bottle. "Do you know she wants me to work for her this summer? It's bad enough she's my mom. Now she's my boss too. Absolute misery."

. . .

Mom was at the dining room table when I got home.

"That's amazing," she was saying to Dad. "Well, let's keep pushing it."

"Keeping pushing what?" I asked.

"Oh hi, sweetie," Mom said. "Your dad figured out that when a story on the Internet mentions both you and me, the click rate doubles and the bounce rate goes down—what was it?"

"Thirty-seven percent," Dad said. "And searches for *Jane Dooley daughter football* are higher than *Jane Dooley mayor, Jane Dooley taxes,* or *Jane Dooley parks.*"

"Is that good?" I asked.

"Well, traffic to our website has tripled since the interview."

"Wow. Imagine if I make the team. You could run for president."

"What's wrong, Tessa?" Mom asked. "I thought we were being excited for each other."

"Are you really excited for me? Or are you excited because of your web . . . whatever Dad was talking about."

"Both!" Mom said. She was standing in front of me now, hands on my shoulders, looking me in the eye. "Sweetie," she said, "if something about the campaign is bothering you, we have to talk. Come doorbelling with me next week, and I promise we'll work it out. The last thing I want is for you to be unhappy. Your happiness is more important than any click rates or voter polls."

"So if I want to talk to you, I have to go doorbelling? We can't just have a conversation at home like a normal family?"

"Okay," Mom said. "What do you want to talk about?"

"I want to know what you really think about me playing football. If you weren't running for mayor, what would you say?"

"I guess I would say I'm confused," Mom admitted. "I don't understand why you want to invest time in something that is dangerous and might not happen, when you have such a bright future as a runner."

"Then why don't you say that?" I asked. "You've never paid attention to anything I've done."

"Tessa, I am not going to make a public statement about whether I think my daughter should play football. That's between us. And of course I care about your extracurricular activities. But you put me in a corner when you told the reporter during my interview that you want to play football. Who is going to vote for the mother who takes away her daughter's dream?"

"It doesn't play well," Dad agreed.

"But between you and me," Mom went on, "I think it's a bad idea. You could get hurt. You might be ostracized. And there's a good chance you'd end up standing on the sideline instead of actually competing. And, to be honest, I'm not even sure the school district will allow it."

"Well, if you're mayor, you can just tell them to allow it."

"It doesn't work that way, Tessa," Dad said. "The school district is governed by a volunteer board that oversees—"

Mom shot Dad a look. I hated that look. Who did she think she was, telling me what I couldn't play and telling Dad when he couldn't speak? She really was a dictator.

"Anyway," Mom said. "We already agreed you'd be focused on the campaign this summer. It'll help me out, and you'll learn so much."

"About waving signs?" I asked.

"It's all part of the experience. We have to think about the future."

Whose future? I wondered. *Mine? Or yours?*

Chapter Twenty-Four
→ CALEB

WEDNESDAY, JUNE 15

One morning during the first week of summer vacation, my phone buzzed before my alarm, which was set for ten o'clock. I was still in bed with a pillow over my head to block the sunlight blazing through the window. I felt blindly on the floor until my fingers came across the phone inside a sneaker.

It was Dobie. "You want to do something?" he asked.

"Yeah," I said. "Sleep."

"Can I come over? I'm stuck at my dad's. I don't want to be here."

"Sure," I said.

By the time I got downstairs, Dobie was already in the kitchen with Luke. They were both eating cereal.

"What's up? You good?" I asked.

"I am now," he said. "Thanks. I had to get out of there."

"Lydia?" I asked, pouring myself a bowl of Cheerios.

"Everything," Dobie said. "Day started with my dad yelling at my mom because she wouldn't sign the football permission slip, and then Lydia yelling at my dad because he got the wrong kind of air freshener. I don't know. Can we just go do something?"

"What do you want to do?"

Dobie pointed to the football on the kitchen table. "Think we can get a game together?"

"Like a real game?"

"Anything. Just for fun."

"I'm in," I said.

"Can I play?" Luke asked.

I nodded. "Ask Charlie too," I said.

Luke tilted his head toward the ceiling. "Charlie! Football!"

"Helpful," I said, swiping my phone on. I sent a message to Nick. *Football.*

He wrote back almost immediately. *When?*

It didn't take long to get a game going. With Luke, Charlie, Nick, Dobie, and me, we had five. We got Roy, Fish, Julian, and Shane next. "That's nine," I said.

"We need one more," Dobie said. "Where's everyone else?"

He meant the other guys from the flag football team. "Gone, I guess. Vacation, camp, sleeping," I said, scrolling through my list.

"Your girlfriend plays football," Luke said. "Call her."

I had to stop and let what Luke had just said sink in. First, I had to start getting used to other people knowing. It was like I wasn't just Caleb anymore. Not that I didn't like it. I wondered what sounded better—Tessa and Caleb, or Caleb and Tessa. Second, Luke seemed surprisingly casual about the fact that she played football. Maybe that was a sign that it wasn't such a huge deal after all. Inviting her to play just for fun could be a way to clear the air between us without sending a message that I thought she should come to camp or tryouts in the fall.

"You cool with that?" I asked Dobie.

"It's just for today, right?" he asked.

"Yeah, totally," I said.

"Because, the other thing—her playing on the team— bad idea, dude."

"Oh, I know. I don't think she really wants to do it," I said with a gulp.

After breakfast, Dobie and I walked to Boardman Park, where we'd made plans to meet everyone else, including Tessa. Charlie was driving Luke in his truck.

"Man, I love summer," I said as we made our way along the river trail. I watched two kayakers paddling in the light rapids. "Do you realize that a week ago at this time we were taking a math test?"

CHAPTER TWENTY-FIVE

→ TESSA

I almost ate my phone when I got the text from Caleb. He wanted me to play football! Not that I needed his permission, but it was such a relief to know he was seeing things differently. I drank a smoothie and ran as fast as I could to the field. I had to escape the house before I got forced into licking envelopes.

I had been so obsessed with not being able to play football that I had forgotten what it was actually like to hold one. When I ran, I lived for the zone—that point in a race when the rhythm comes automatically, my feet flying over roots, dirt, and rocks, while my eyes stay locked on the trees, the sky, or whatever sucker I'm about to pass. I felt all that when I ran a good route in football, but the cherry on top was the sensation of catching a perfectly thrown ball in stride and sprinting away from the defensive back I was about to burn for six. That was why I was like a kid on cake when the game started.

There were just enough of us for a real game. It was Caleb, Dobie, Luke, Shane, and me in pinnies against Nick, Charlie, Roy, Fish, and Julian in shirts.

We stood in a circle near the middle of the field. "All right, dorks," Charlie said. "This is two-hand touch, two completions. No runs. Touchdown is the full seven." He paused. "What else? Oh yeah, blitz count is ten Boise Idaho. And remember we've got a girl out here."

"Hey," I said. "I can handle myself."

Charlie smiled and pointed at Luke. "I was talking about him."

"I'll remember that," Luke said, coming up a little short of threatening.

"You should," I told him. "It's a compliment."

"Who starts?" Caleb asked.

Charlie held up the football. "Losers walk," he said.

"We haven't lost anything yet," Caleb replied confidently.

Charlie was just as confident as Caleb. "You will," he replied.

I could see where Caleb got it, like it was hand-me-down swagger.

My team hustled to the other end of the field.

Charlie raised his hand. "Ready?"

I raised my hand. "Ready!"

He let the football fly. I sidestepped to my right until I was under it. After a clean catch, I tucked the ball away and found a seam up the sideline. I shifted into a higher gear, trying to cover as much ground as I could before the defense closed in on me. I was fifteen yards up when I heard the two sweetest words a girl can hear when playing with all boys on the football field.

"Get her!"

I think it was Roy yelling at Julian. Whoever said it, it was like sprinkling turbo dust onto a video game player. I ran from the voice behind me, still clutching the football, until Charlie ended my kickoff return with a two-handed tag.

"That was friggin' spectacular," Caleb said, holding up his hands.

"Bam," I replied, slapping his hands.

"Bam," he said.

Dobie looked at us impatiently. "Hey, uh, you two want to keeping playing, or was that enough for one day?" We joined him and Luke in the huddle.

I could have stayed in a huddle for hours. I loved it. There was always either too much energy or everyone was wiped out. Even if it was cold, a cloud of sweat and dust hung overhead. The QB talked first, and nobody ever questioned anything, even if the play made no sense, which I enjoyed, especially when the QB was me. And we all talked like we were about to invade a foreign country.

Dobie drew up the first play on his finger. From what I could tell, I was supposed to run a slant route left to right across the field and he'd hit me in stride. Luke would try to lose Roy with a hitch, then run deep. Caleb was the checkdown option, hanging closer in case nobody got open.

Dobie turned his hand over so it was palm down. "Ready?" he asked.

"Let's do it," said Caleb.

We stacked our hands, then broke the huddle.

Julian lined up across from me. I didn't know much about Julian except that he went to Caleb's school. But one look told me everything. The attitude. The fitted long-sleeved undershirt. The bright red shoes. He was the star of his own highlight reel. He had probably burned half the guys in town in four sports. But I could see from the look on his face that he had no idea what to do with me.

"You can't win," I said. "Play off me or jam me. I'll take you deep either way."

"I don't think so," Julian said.

"You don't think so?" I repeated. "That's all you got?"

Julian shook his head. "Not gonna happen."

"Let's talk about it in the end zone," I said.

Roy jogged by Julian. "Careful, dude. She's got wheels."

Julian backed away from the line. "No problem," he replied.

Chapter Twenty-Six

CALEB

I will say this. If there was any girl who could play high school football, it was Tessa. She was fast, ran good routes, and could catch. But there was one more thing about her that nobody else knew: she was lethal with head games. She had Julian completely out of his game. He was so afraid of Tessa beating him deep that he just assumed she was running a straight fly route. Dude never considered she was going to break inside on a slant.

And she nailed it.

Once Julian bit on the go route, it was game over. Tessa went zero to sixty up the left sideline, with Julian on the outside. Suddenly she hit the brakes and broke to her right. Julian got his feet crossed up trying to stay with her. He stumbled just as Tessa caught the ball in stride and turned upfield.

That wasn't football. That was artwork.

Dobie, Luke, Shane, and I watched Tessa cross the line

into the end zone. "I don't think *plays like a girl* means what we think it does," Dobie said.

"Depends on the girl, I guess," Luke replied.

"After that, maybe we should change it to *plays like a Julian*," I said, just loud enough for Julian to hear.

"All right, all right," he said. "I got beat by a girl. You all happy?"

"Dude, you didn't get beat by a girl," Roy said. "You just got *beat*." Roy walked up to Tessa. "I don't care what locker room you use," he added. "That was slick."

The game lasted almost two hours.

In the end, my team lost by a touchdown. Tessa had gotten the best of Julian, but she couldn't stop him either. He was flat-out faster than she was. On offense, she could make up for that by running good routes, but on defense, Julian's speed was a problem for her.

"You're lucky it wasn't tackle," Charlie said to my team.

"I wish it was," Dobie said. Big mistake.

Charlie smiled. He tossed Dobie the football. "You want to play some tackle?"

Dobie nodded. "Bring it."

Without warning, Charlie barreled into Dobie, hitting him square in the chest and knocking him six feet back onto his butt.

We all cheered. Dobie sat up slowly. "That was awesome."

"Do me!" Roy yelled.

Charlie plowed into Roy, flattening him.

Roy rolled onto his side, clutching his ribs. "Feels great."

One by one we all took turns getting tackled by Charlie.

Before long the field looked like the set of a kung-fu movie. There was only one person who Charlie hadn't tackled.

"My turn," Tessa said, standing about ten feet from Charlie.

Charlie shook his head. "Not today," he replied. I knew from the tone of his voice that he wasn't going to change his mind.

Tessa waved her hand at the guys. "You tackled everyone else."

"That's different," Charlie explained.

"Because I'm a girl?"

"No, because I'm a guy."

CHAPTER TWENTY-SEVEN

↳TESSA

After the game, Caleb and I went to town for frozen yogurt.

"Why wouldn't your brother tackle me?" I asked him. We were sitting on stools at a counter by the window facing the street.

Caleb dug his pink plastic spoon into a bowl of black-berry yogurt. "What did he say?"

"Seriously, Caleb? You were right there."

"I forgot."

"He said *because I'm a guy.* I want to know what he meant."

"I guess it's like this: If Charlie tackles me and I get hurt, we all laugh and he tells me to rub some dirt on it. I mean, even if he broke one of my ribs, he'd be right behind me in the hospital telling me to walk it off. But if the same thing happens and it's you, nobody's laughing."

"I can take it," I said.

"Maybe," Caleb said carefully. "But Charlie can't."

"Can't what?"

"Handle it."

"Handle what? I don't get it."

"Charlie works at a gym with a bunch of meatheads. He couldn't handle being the guy who hurt a girl. And that goes for most of us. No matter how it happens. It's nothing against you or any other girl. It's just the way we are. Some of us, anyway."

"Stop it," I said. "That's crazy."

"It's the truth," Caleb said. "Sorry if you don't like it."

"Let me get this straight. First everyone says I can't play football because I might get hurt. Now I can't play football because if I get hurt, it would make you guys *feel* bad? That's pathetic and you need to get over it."

"I can't just get over it, Tessa. It's, like, how I'm programmed. Guys I know don't hit girls. They don't tackle girls. They just don't. This is what I've been trying to tell you. You can come to football camp. And if you try out for the football team, you might be better than a lot of the guys out there. But don't be surprised if nobody touches you."

"Because you're all chickens."

"Can you blame us?"

Yes, I could blame them! What a stupid, stupid, stupid question. I was fighting against injustice, discrimination, and dumb rules enforced in the name of tradition. They were making a choice to be afraid of nothing and acting like the whole situation was just as bad for them as it was for me. Why couldn't they say what they were really feeling? That they were afraid of getting outplayed by a girl?

118

After a couple of minutes of silence where we both just swirled our spoons around in our empty frozen yogurt bowls, I finally asked Caleb a question. "Would it make you feel better if I told you there were zero other girls in Pilchuck who wanted to play football?"

Caleb just looked at me.

"I'm it, dude," I said. "There's nobody else behind me. The girls are not going to take over your football team. We're going to keep playing all the other sports and going to piano lessons and babysitting after school. So maybe you can just quit being so paranoid and relax long enough to give me some respect."

CHAPTER TWENTY-EIGHT
→ CALEB

"Wow, she really let you have it, huh?" Charlie asked as he rolled the hot dogs on the grill and then took a sip of his soda.

"Don't laugh," I said. "It's your fault."

"How is it my fault?"

"You wouldn't tackle her."

"Oh, come on," Charlie replied. "You and I both know what that was about."

"Is it because you're afraid of what people would say if you tackled a girl?"

"Pretty much. Caleb, I'm a twenty-year-old guy. I'm six two. I weigh two hundred and twenty-five pounds. I work at a gym. If I laid a hand on that girl, I'd probably go to jail. You want to come visit me in jail?"

"No."

"Then shut up about it. Look, if she wants to play football, fine. But that doesn't mean everyone has to like it."

"I know."

"Is she still your girlfriend?"

"Beats me. I mean, we do stuff together."

Charlie raised one eyebrow. "What kind of stuff?"

"Like go out for frozen yogurt."

"Do you want her to be your girlfriend?"

"I like her."

"But?"

"It's complicated," I said. "It's okay right now, but I guess I'm kind of afraid of this turning into a thing when I get to high school and it's like, *There goes the guy going out with the football girl.* I don't want to be known as the guy going out with the football girl. The guy going out with Tessa Dooley or the guy going out with the mayor's daughter, I can handle that. Not the football girl. What would you do?"

"I think she's got a choice to make. It's either you or football. I know that sounds harsh, but listen to the voice in your head and tell me I'm wrong."

I knew Charlie was right. I did want Tessa to make a choice. I just didn't want her to choose football. I liked her. I liked that she liked me. I wanted people in high school to look at us and say, *Oh, there go Caleb and Tessa.* Or Tessa and Caleb. I didn't really care whose name came first. And I could never say this to her, but when I pictured us in the future, she wasn't sitting next to me on the bench with a mouth guard covering her teeth. She was sitting in the stands cheering for me.

Was that so terrible?

.   .   .

Charlie and I were eating our hot dogs on the back porch when Mom and Dad came home from the shop. I could see them through the window. Dad moved stiffly to the kitchen table and sat down. Mom set a glass of water on the table, along with two pills.

"You should take a day off," Mom said.

Dad grunted. "It's summer, Janet. You know we're stacked. I can't walk away from the business."

"If you don't take it easy, you're not going to be walking away from anything. Why don't you bring someone on part-time to help? We can afford it."

Charlie looked over at me. "Here we go," he said quietly.

I thought about making a noise so Mom and Dad would know we could hear them, but I froze. I braced myself for Dad's answer to Mom's idea about hiring someone to help them.

"I shouldn't have to hire anyone," he said. "This is a family business. The problem is, not everyone in the family seems to get that."

"Give him space, Tom," Mom said. "He's finding his way."

"Well, I don't think he should be doing it in this house. He knows what the deal is. If he wants to lift weights for a living, he can pay his own rent." The next thing we saw was Mom following Dad out of the kitchen.

"What's he talking about?" I asked Charlie.

Charlie chucked his empty soda can toward the recycling bin. "He gave me a choice. I can work at the shop or move out. I have to decide by the end of July."

"Seriously?" I asked. "That's not fair. You have a job."

"Not the right job," Charlie replied.

"Why can't you work both places?"

"Because it's not just work, Caleb. I'm applying to a program."

"What kind of program?"

"Physical therapy. Well, first I have to take a bunch of classes before I officially start the program. But if I get in, I'm going to do it."

"Here?"

Charlie shook his head silently. "Spokane."

"Spokane? That's on the other side of the state. Why would you go there?"

"That's where the program is."

"So find another one."

"Caleb, come on."

"No, find another one. This is crap. You can't just leave."

"Dude, I'm too old to be living at home. Dad's right about that. Look around. Do any of your other friends have deadbeat brothers in their twenties hanging around the house?" Charlie smiled. "It's kind of pathetic."

"It's not pathetic," I said, standing up. "What's pathetic is that you think you're too good to work at the aluminum siding company. But you know what, don't worry about it. Luke and I got it. You go to Spokane and do whatever you want. We'll be fine without you."

"I know you will," Charlie said tiredly.

I left the back porch, heading for the woods behind the house, but not before hurling two more words at Charlie. "You suck."

CHAPTER TWENTY-NINE
→ TESSA

THURSDAY, JUNE 16

After the worst frozen yogurt date in the history of human civilization, it was pretty obvious that I needed someone to talk to. I needed my friends.

My hands trembled as I texted Marina and Lexie.

Can we hang out? pls. I miss you.

"They're going to make me suffer," I said to the phone. It buzzed right away. I yelped.

run?
def. now?
yes.

Half an hour later, Marina, Lexie, and I were tearing up the trails above Boardman Park. At first, I pretended I was having a hard time keeping up with them. By the second mile, it was no joke. They were smoking me. I wasn't out of shape. I was out of practice. In cross-country, the faster runner didn't always win. There was more to it. Footwork, pacing, passing. I stumbled more than I usually did. On the final downhill stretch, I bit it big-time, and ended up with a raspberry on my thigh.

"Better get that cleaned up," Marina said during our cooldown back in Boardman Park.

I squirted water onto it straight from my bottle. "That'll have to do," I said.

"I don't think I've ever seen you fall like that," Lexie said.

"I missed a step," I replied.

"I'm sure you'll get hurt worse than that playing football," Marina responded.

"You mean if I go to football camp."

"Now it's an *if*?" Lexie asked. "I thought you were done with cross-country."

"I never said that. I said I didn't know what I wanted to do. And I still don't. But I know I want my friends. I need you guys."

"What happened?" Marina asked.

"What do you mean?"

"Tess, nobody texts out of the blue for no reason. Something must have happened. So spill it. What's the drama?"

"Caleb and I had a fight."

"About what?"

"Guess."

"You're kidding me. Is any relationship in your life safe from this sport?"

"Can I just tell you the story, and then you tell me I'm right?" I said with a smile.

"Sure," Marina replied.

"He keeps saying I'm a great football player, but he obviously doesn't want me to actually play. He won't come right out and say it, but every time it comes up, he has a new reason why it's not a good idea. Like, *It's a rough sport, Tessa. You might get hurt.* Or *I'm cool with it, but a lot of the other guys won't be.* Or now it's *Tessa, you don't get how bad it is for a dude's reputation if he tackles a chick.*"

"He said *chick*?"

"Yes," I lied.

Lexie scrunched up her face. "So, tell us again why you won't just run cross-country? Is it still about the catch?"

"You mean the pass I dropped?"

"Sorry, the drop. Oh, and Congress, right?" Lexie added with a smile.

"It is about the drop," I said. "And it's about Congress. Put those things together, and I'm just not in the mood to go with the flow. I'm tired of being invisible and stressing about meeting other people's expectations. I think I have to go my own way, or I won't be happy and I'll make you and everyone else around me miserable. Plus I really like playing football."

"There are other sports," Marina said. "Soccer."

"Meh."

"Lacrosse."

"No."

"Field hockey."

I shook my head.

"Volleyball."

"Stop."

"Play football, then," Marina said. "What's the worst that could happen? I mean, besides injury or death."

"It would change things. With Caleb."

"Well, what do you like more, football or Caleb? If you had to choose."

"If I had to choose? I choose both."

"You just said it would change things."

"Well, maybe it doesn't have to," I said, trying to think positively. "So we had a fight? Who cares? He's probably just worried about me. I bet once he sees me play in an actual game and I don't get hurt, he'll get over it. Hopefully Congress will too. Maybe for once she'll notice and be proud of me."

"Hmm," said Marina.

"You know what I should do? I should definitely show up at that football camp."

"Oh, I don't know," said Lexie.

"It's aggressive. They'll respect that. It'll show them I'm serious. We'll get all the weirdness out of the way, so by the time the season starts, it'll be ancient history and we'll be one big happy team."

"I hope all your dreams come true," Marina said, like she thought I was living in a fantasy world. I could tell she was being sincere, though.

"Thank you. And I'm sorry I wasn't totally honest with you and Lexie before."

"You're forgiven," Lexie said. "You're crazy. But you're forgiven. And we're sorry too. You've never been invisible to us."

Maybe it was crazy, but knowing I had my friends back, I was more tired than ever of worrying about what everyone else thought. It was time to do what I wanted to do. The truth was, I liked being the football girl. It had become my thing. I'd made it happen. Without it I was a face in the crowd, another girl waiting to get noticed, hoping someone would pick her for the team, ask her to the dance, or tell her how smart she was. From now on I wasn't going to ask for permission or say I was sorry or sweat it with Caleb or Mom or anyone else. This was about me catching footballs. Game on.

CHAPTER THIRTY
→ CALEB

THURSDAY, JUNE 23

Summer started slow. I spent a lot of time helping out at the shop. Tessa was always running with her friends. One day I played two-on-two football with Dobie, Nick, and Julian. I must have been off my game, because I couldn't throw straight or catch. The guys called me out when we were done.

"What's wrong with you, dude?" Dobie asked as we sat on the bleachers drinking water in the late-morning sun.

"Nothing," I said. "I just didn't have it today."

"Didn't have it?" Dobie repeated. "You played like a . . ." He stopped himself.

"Like a what?" I asked.

"Like my—my grandmother," Nick stammered.

"No," I said to Dobie. "You were going to say *like a girl*."

"So what?" Dobie said. "It's just an expression."

I twisted the cap onto my half-filled bottle of water and threw the whole thing at Dobie's head.

"Hey!" he said. "What's your problem?"

"Oh, sorry," I said. "It was just an expression."

Dobie stood up. "Do it again," he dared me.

I rose to face him. "Say I played like a girl again," I replied.

Nick jumped in between us. "Take it easy," he said. "I'm sure you're both sorry. Let's just go get Slurpees or something and forget it happened."

"I got a better idea," Dobie said, staring at me. "Why don't the rest of us go get Slurpees, and Caleb can go crying to his girlfriend. Or did she dump you?"

"She didn't dump me," I said.

"That's funny, because I haven't seen her in a while. Is she too busy getting ready for football camp?"

"Shut up, Dobie."

"Do us a favor," Dobie went on. "If you do see her, will you talk some sense into her? Tell her to find her own sport."

It was a good thing Nick was blocking my way, because I was ready to go after Dobie. Dobie hopped off the bleachers and started walking in the other direction. Julian followed him.

"Come on, Nick," Dobie called.

"Don't listen to him," Nick said. "He doesn't mean it. Tessa's cool, man. Dobie's just blowing off steam."

I nodded. "If you say so."

Nick followed Dobie and Julian away from the park while I stayed on the bleachers by myself. The fight with

Dobie didn't bother me. Dobie had a temper and liked to get under my skin. We'd be fine. But I realized I did really want to see Tessa. Not to talk sense into her, whatever that meant. I just missed her. Nothing was as much fun when she wasn't around. I hoped this football thing would be over soon so we could hang out the way we used to.

CHAPTER THIRTY-ONE

→ TESSA

FRIDAY, JULY 1

I had this crazy idea that if I left Caleb alone, he would decide on his own that he was making a big deal out of nothing. He did not have to worry about me or choose between me and football. We could be more than one thing to each other at the same time. In my mind he'd show up on my doorstep and say he liked me whether I was the football girl or not. So I waited for him to call, or text, or ring the bell.

In the meantime, Mom's campaign was going well. Mom stuck to her main issues. If someone asked her about me, she would say "I'm proud of my daughter" without saying why. I wished she could come up with one reason, even if it had nothing to do with football. There were more people every day around the house. Volunteers mostly, who came to make phone calls, put up signs around town, or stuff envelopes.

Dad put me in charge of watching social media for anyone talking about Mom. It was an easy job. I set up alerts for *Jane Dooley, Councilwoman Dooley,* and *Mayor Dooley* and waited for my phone to buzz. Dad acted like I was saving the world.

"Great catch!" he'd say whenever I showed him a tweet or post that mentioned Mom. "Let's capture that."

Dad never told me exactly what he meant by that, so I just took screenshots and saved them to my gallery. Every few hours, he would call me over and show me a graph with yellow, green, and red lines that went up and down. It reminded me of a hospital monitor.

"Is Mom dying?" I finally asked, nibbling on a rice cake.

Dad frowned at me. "These are analytics," he explained. "See. You can tell how many times people are going to the campaign website throughout the day, how long they're staying there, and what pages they're reading."

"So you're spying on them?"

"We're learning from them," Dad said. "What they like. What they don't like. If we post a video and nobody watches it, we take it down. If lots of people click on it, we move it to the front of the website."

I would never admit Mom was right, but I was learning something. I'd always thought Dad made a big deal over the numbers because he just wanted people to like Mom. I could see now that it was really about getting people to listen to her.

"Why is the green line going up here?" I asked, pointing at the screen.

"I'm not sure," Dad said, squinting. "Why don't you check into it?"

"Me?"

"Would you, please?" he asked. "I need to meet with some of the volunteers."

I studied the graph and figured out that the green line showed how many clicks Mom's tweets were getting. It looked like mountains and valleys. Up meant more clicks, down meant less. I checked out the popular tweets and saw that they all had photos. That made sense. Who didn't like photos? When I pointed this out to Dad, he whacked me on the back so hard, I almost fell over. "Fantastic, Tessa!" he said, before hugging me.

I smiled as Dad wrapped me up in his arms. I couldn't remember the last time that had happened. Even if he was proud of me for something that was more important to him than it was to me, it still felt good.

Finally, right before the Fourth of July, Caleb texted me.

Wanna hang.

Is that a ? Never mind. Sure. Come over tomorrow.

Cool.

Chapter Thirty-Two

➔ CALEB

SATURDAY, JULY 2

Tessa's dad showed me through the house and out the back door. The first thing he did was hand me a staple gun. "Just fire a couple of these into the wooden stakes and toss it there," he said, pointing to a stack of signs piled up on the deck.

"Sure, Mr. Dooley," I said.

"Call me Alan."

"Okay, um, Alan."

I started stapling signs. Tessa was at the picnic table stuffing envelopes. After a few minutes her mom came outside.

"Hi, Caleb," she said. "Thanks so much for helping today."

She sat at the picnic table and opened her laptop.

"My pleasure, Mrs. Dooley."

"Oh, please," she said. "Call me Mayor Dooley."

"That would be pretty cool," I said.

"Too bad you can't vote," she said.

"He wouldn't vote for you, Mom," replied Tessa.

"What makes you say that?" she asked.

"Because you're a Democrat. And he's a Republican."

I was surprised Tessa said that. I wasn't even sure it was true. My dad was a Republican, and I was pretty sure Charlie was too. But I wasn't really anything. I'd run for student council last year, but the only thing I'd stood for was bigger lunches.

There was a sharp edge in Tessa's voice. I didn't want to be in the middle of a fight with her mom, so I tried to say something that would make them both happy.

"I might vote for her," I said. "I can be open-minded."

"You know she wants to raise taxes?" Tessa asked.

"For our schools," Mrs. Dooley added. "And technically the mayor doesn't raise taxes. The state does. But I support using taxes for our schools."

"But not the football stadium," Tessa added. "Even though everyone else in the town wants it."

"In a perfect world, we'd all have everything we wanted," Mrs. Dooley said to me. "But that isn't the way it works."

"I don't think my dad wants a new stadium," I said. "He really doesn't like paying for anything. But he likes football."

"Tessa says you're a good athlete, Caleb," Mrs. Dooley said. "Are you going to play football this fall?"

"I'm going to try out," I said. "And there's a football camp this summer me and my friends are going to do."

"That sounds great," Mrs. Dooley said.

Tessa tossed a stack of envelopes into a box on the ground. "I might do it too," she said casually. "Remember? I talked about it during the interview?"

"Do what, sweetie?" Mrs. Dooley asked.

"The football camp."

Mrs. Dooley looked over at Tessa and frowned. "We can talk about it later."

Tessa kept going. "Remember how you said you were proud of me, and how you wanted me to be successful? Or did you just mean successful in a way that helps you?"

"You're taking both comments out of context," Mrs. Dooley answered. "I also told you I didn't think it was a good idea."

"You know you can get concussions in any sport?" Tessa asked.

"It's not just about concussions, Tessa."

I listened to Tessa and her mom go back and forth, and only one thought went through my head. *Please don't ask me what I think. Please don't ask me what I think.* Because I would have to either lie or tell Tessa that I agreed with her mom.

I left that day without actually talking to Tessa. But I'd have to be deaf to think she had changed her mind about anything. The tone of her voice told me she was more determined than ever to play football. It was totally Tessa, and it made me like her even more than before. I just wished I could tell her that deep down, I didn't see any way this could end well for her or for us.

. . .

Everyone was home for dinner that night. Mom made Dad close the shop early even though it was still light, Charlie had a day off from the gym, and Luke had nothing better to do.

"Hope you're hungry," Mom said as she started bringing food to the table. Chili dogs, corn on the cob, potato salad, green beans, and watermelon.

There wasn't much chatter for a while. We were too busy eating. At one point, Luke was two-fisting a slice of watermelon and a chili dog. I was pretty sure I saw him spit out a bean and a seed at the same time.

"This is great, Mom," Charlie said at last. "I'm going to miss your chili dogs."

Mom smiled. "I can tell you how to make them."

"It won't be the same," Charlie replied.

"Have you found a place to live?" Dad asked.

He lives here, I thought, unsure who to be mad at—Dad for pushing Charlie out or Charlie for letting it happen.

"I've got a few leads," Charlie said.

"You know, other than college I've only lived in two places," Dad said. "My parents' house and this house."

"Good story, Dad," Luke said.

"It might sound boring to you, Luke, but the way I saw it, sticking with what I knew was better than searching aimlessly for something new."

Charlie put his glass down hard enough to rattle the table. "Dad, starting a program five hours away is not searching

138

aimlessly. I have a plan. Physical therapy is a real thing. And I think I can be really good at it."

"I'm not going to argue with you, Charlie," Dad said. "You've made up your mind. You're leaving. We'll be here. And we'll be fine." He looked over at me. "Right, Caleb?"

I wasn't sure what Dad meant by that. He might have been talking about the next few years of high school and football for me and for Luke. On the other hand, knowing how Dad felt about change, what he'd said made me wonder if he was thinking of a future where Luke and I would be running the business. That was a little scary. For the first time, I could understand why someone would want to take a chance on something new when they could, even if everyone else was telling them they were nuts.

CHAPTER THIRTY-THREE

→ TESSA

SUNDAY, JULY 3

The next day, Mom and I drove across town to the developments with the new homes. Wide sidewalks, brightly painted houses, green lawns, and neatly mulched gardens. Everything was just a little too perfect.

"Oh, look!" Mom said, pointing to a large brown house. "There's one." She looked in her rearview mirror and smiled.

"One what?" I turned around in my seat. Whatever it was, I'd missed it.

"A campaign sign," Mom replied. "'Jane Dooley for Mayor.'"

"Guess we can skip that house, then," I said.

"Ha ha," Mom replied, coming to a stop in front of a small park.

To my surprise, Beth was standing on the sidewalk with

the cameraman. Mom and I both got out of the car smiling, but for different reasons.

"Hi!" Mom said. "I'm so glad you could join us."

"Me too," said Beth. "Tessa, it's nice to see you again."

Mom ended up doing most of the doorbelling herself. That meant I was really going on a walk with Beth.

"So are you excited about high school?" she asked.

"Kind of," I said.

"Would you really like to be on the football team?" she asked. "Just between us."

"I want to try."

"But they won't let you?"

"No, it's not that. I think they have to let me." I told her about the research I'd done.

"So what's holding you back?"

It was so tempting to tell Beth that my mother would not let me play football, that she was only going along with this whole charade because it made her look good. As long as Mom was the star of the show, it didn't matter what I did, and that was what bugged me. She would look like a giant hypocrite if *that* was in the newspaper. Her slogan was *Own the day!* The only thing that stopped me from telling Beth all this was the knowledge that I still needed Mom to sign the permission slip for football camp, which started in two weeks.

"Nothing, really."

"Your friend plays football too, right?"

"Yeah, Caleb."

"What does he think of all this?"

"He told me I should do it. And he kind of told me I shouldn't. He's been a little unclear on the issue."

"What about his friends?"

"I don't really know. I haven't asked him."

"Any chance they're a little afraid of you? I mean, let's say you try out and you're great. You could take a spot away from one of the guys. That would be tough to live down for a teenage boy—losing their spot to a girl."

I laughed. "Yeah, they should be afraid."

Beth laughed too. "Can I quote you on that?"

"What do you mean, like for the news? On TV?"

"This wouldn't be on TV," Beth said. "I also write stories for the *Pilchuck Observer*."

I looked at Mom, who was charming an older couple. She had been talking to them the whole time Beth and I had been chatting. I realized how hard she was working and how badly she wanted to be mayor. Why couldn't she look at me and see how badly I wanted to play football? "Sure," I said to Beth, deciding it was time to speak up. "You can quote me."

CHAPTER THIRTY-FOUR

→ CALEB

SATURDAY, JULY 9

"Dude, this has to stop."

Aaron Parker pointed to a tweet on his phone. We were standing in front of the rec center, where Dobie and I had come to shoot hoops. Enough time had gone by since my argument with Dobie. We were over it.

> @PilchuckObserver. The football girl has a message for the boys: Be afraid.

There was a link to an article.

I didn't need to read the rest of it.

"Maybe she didn't say it exactly like that," I guessed. "Sometimes people's words get twisted around in the media."

Aaron didn't buy it. "Listen, we have a chance to be

really good this year. We don't want her getting in the way of that."

"How does one girl get in the way of anything?" I asked. "I mean, she might not even make the team."

"It's a distraction," Aaron answered, sounding reasonable. "Coach says our job is to focus on winning football games. How are we supposed to do that if everyone's talking about the football girl? You know, if her mom is the mayor, we'll never get a new football stadium?"

"I guess," I said. I thought about pointing out to Aaron that the only people distracted by Tessa were the people who didn't want her on the team. But I also didn't feel right arguing with him. I was the new guy. The rookie. Aaron was a big deal on the team, and I wanted to stay on his good side.

"So you'll talk to her?"

"Yeah, okay."

Aaron held out his fist. "You're a champ, McCleary," he said. "It'll be better this way. She'll find her own thing, and you'll be on your way to the big time." Then he left me alone.

I went inside, wondering if *the big time* meant the same thing to me that it did to Aaron. I had a feeling that for Aaron *the big time* was starting on varsity, winning games, district, state. I'd be a star. I'd get my picture in the paper, and Dad would frame the picture to hang on the wall in the shop to prove that the McCleary family tradition lived on. College coaches would call. It all sounded great. But I didn't know if that was exactly what I wanted.

· · ·

Late that night, I got up to go to the bathroom. The light was on in Charlie's room. I hadn't seen him for a week. I peeked inside. The bed was stripped. There were boxes stacked against the wall. Suddenly it hit home. This was really happening. Charlie was leaving. For a moment, I was actually afraid he was already gone.

I found Charlie in the kitchen spreading peanut butter on crackers and then popping them into his mouth one by one like it was the only thing he really wanted to do with his life.

"Eat much?" I asked.

Charlie swore. "You scared me," he said.

"Why is all your stuff in boxes?"

"I'm out," Charlie answered, like he'd given up. "I found a place in Spokane. I'm moving in next week. It's faster than I thought, but I gotta do it. I was going to tell you."

"When?"

"Tomorrow. Today. Whatever time this makes it."

I grabbed a handful of crackers, and Charlie passed me the peanut butter. After eating a few, I could see why he seemed so calm. Peanut butter slowed everything down. It was hard to get upset. Anyway, I knew there was no fighting this. Charlie was leaving.

"I don't know what to do," I said.

"You put the knife into the jar and then spread it across the cracker," Charlie said with a straight face.

"Not that." Then I told him about my conversation with Aaron.

"I don't know, man," Charlie said. "I feel like whatever

I say is going to be wrong, because all I can say is what I would do, and I'm right less than half the time."

"What would you do?"

"What are your options?"

"I guess I can either tell Tessa to give it up or I can let her do what she wants to do."

Charlie laughed so hard, bits of cracker flew across the table. "Sorry, dude. But I think you just answered your own question."

"What do you mean?"

"That first option is a joke. What do you think will happen if you tell Tessa to give it up?" Charlie put *tell* in air quotes. "I saw the tweet. She's made it pretty clear she means business. I don't think she's going to let anyone talk her out of this now."

"Yeah, I don't know. She'd probably ignore me."

"Right. So you really only have one option."

"Let her do what she wants to do."

"Pretty much, bro."

That was not what I wanted to hear. I could see it from Tessa's point of view, but that didn't mean I liked it. I had hoped Charlie would tell me that, yeah, Tessa had a right to pursue her dream, but it wasn't fair for her to do it at my expense. "What do I tell Aaron?"

"Tell him whatever you want," Charlie said. "Tell him you tried but she wouldn't listen. Tell him it's a free country. Tell him if he hates the idea of having a girl on the team, he should try a new sport himself."

"Ha! He'll love that."

"Look, here's all I can say. When we were talking on that camping trip, you were juiced. I could see it. This girl matters to you. I've never seen you so lovestruck over football."

"I'm not lovestruck," I said.

Charlie held his thumb and pointer finger an inch apart. "Little bit."

We munched on crackers without saying anything for a few minutes. Eventually Charlie went to the fridge and came back with a carton of milk, which we passed back and forth without using glasses.

"Mom would kill us," I said.

"This is easier," Charlie answered. "I think I'm going to like living alone."

"How do you know you're doing the right thing?" I asked. "What if this doesn't work out?"

"There's always a chance it won't work if I go," Charlie said. "But there's a hundred percent chance it won't work if I don't."

"You know I suck at math," I said.

"My gut says go," Charlie said. "Is that better?"

"Can I come with you?"

"Man, that would be great," Charlie said with a smile. "The McCleary brothers staying up all night eating peanut butter and crackers. Too bad I won't be able to afford cable."

"I'm staying," I said.

Charlie raised the milk carton. "Cheers, man. I'm gonna miss you. I'll be home to visit before you know it."

CHAPTER THIRTY-FIVE

→ TESSA

WEDNESDAY, JULY 13

There was a blank permission slip for football camp folded in a book on my desk. I'd picked it up at the rec center so I could give it to Mom to sign when I finally found the nerve to ask her. I had to move fast, though. Football camp started in a few days.

One crazy hot morning a few days after I lost the nerve again to ask Mom to sign the form, Marina and I went to the Verlot Street bridge to wave signs at cars passing by. Lexie would have come with us, but she hated the heat.

I figured if I did enough to get Mom elected mayor, she might do me a favor and let me go to football camp.

"Isn't the election in November?" Marina asked.

"Jane says she has to make an early impression," I said, drawing out Mom's name like it belonged to someone very important.

Marina and I worked the bridge for most of the morning. We'd lean over the rail and wave, and whenever a car honked, we'd jump up and down. I'm sure we looked loopy, but it was fun, even though we weren't getting paid and my eyebrows were melting off my face. When the heat got too intense, we sat in the shade and gulped water.

"So, what else is new?" Marina asked, like she had something on her mind.

"Have I been unpleasant?" I blurted. It wasn't something I'd planned to ask. But it was suddenly something I had to know.

"Define *unpleasant*," Marina said carefully.

"Selfish. Mean. Murderous."

"I wouldn't say you've been mean."

"Just selfish and murderous?"

"Maybe a little bit selfish," Marina answered. "But I forgive you. You seem remorseful."

"I am sorry," I said, looking at Marina. "I guess I've been thinking about myself a lot this summer."

"Well, that is the definition of *selfish*."

"I wish I could snap my fingers and everything complicated going on in my life would disappear and it would all be normal and boring."

"Liar," said Marina.

"Okay, but I am sorry," I repeated.

"Don't feel bad. You just have a wicked case of Caleb fever."

"Marina!"

"He fried your brain, Tessa. You can plead insanity."

"You're a liar!" I said, laughing and yelling at the same time. "That boy did not fry this girl's brain."

"Then what's the whole football thing about?"

"I'll tell you as long as you swear this is just two girls talking about football, okay? No boys."

"No boys," Marina promised.

"I can still see the ball coming toward me," I said.

Marina buried her head in her hands. "Oh, why did I ask?"

"Give me a chance to finish," I told Marina. "It's not about one play. It was, at first. Now it's like . . . Have you ever gone to a restaurant and you knew you wanted the fish taco, until someone said 'You should get the fish taco,' and suddenly you didn't want the fish taco at all? You wanted the burger. That's how I feel. People have always been telling me to order the fish tacos, and now I am finally ordering the burger I want because, screw them, it's my life."

"What if you order the burger and you don't like it, and then it's too late because the fish tacos are all gone?"

"I guess I hadn't thought about it like that. And anyway, it's a little late now," I said.

"What do you mean?"

I showed Marina the "be afraid" tweet. "I kind of threw it down. Publicly."

"I saw it," Marina said. "But I promise I didn't retweet it. I was afraid."

"So am I," I said.

"What do you mean? The tweet was quoting what you said."

"But what if you're right? What if I choose football and it's all wrong and I can't go back?"

Marina shrugged. "What if you choose cross-country and you spend the rest of high school wondering what would have happened if you had chosen football?"

I didn't have any answers. All I could think was that life would be simpler if I had never touched a football. Still, it felt good to really talk with Marina. I was doing something *I* wanted to do, not to please someone else. Before we left, I took a picture of us on the bridge and sent it to Lexie with a note.

Marina says she really forgives me. Do you?

Lexie wrote back.

Do I have a choice? ☺

Chapter Thirty-Six

→ CALEB

It was late in the evening on the day Charlie officially moved out. I was in the living room, flipping through one of Charlie's·old playbooks, when Dad walked in with two ice cream sandwiches.

"You want one?" he asked.

"Sure," I said.

We ate in silence for a few moments.

"How you doing?" he asked me at last.

"Good," I said. "I guess."

"I miss him too," Dad replied. "You know that, right?"

I couldn't honestly tell him that I did. I think he knew it. He exhaled, a little sadly, and said, "Yeah. I can see how it looked. I lost my patience. You get ideas about choices you want someone to make, and you forget whose choices they are." Dad looked me in the eye. "The truth is, I'm proud of your brother for believing in himself. He's going to be great at whatever he does. And so are you, Caleb. Your job now is to have some fun, play hard, and do your homework." He smiled. "I reversed the order."

"Can we visit him?" I asked.

"You bet," Dad said. "I'd like that."

The text from Aaron Parker came about an hour later.

Outside in five. Let's have some fun.

It was a little past nine. The house was quiet. Luke was at a friend's house. Mom and Dad were upstairs watching a movie. They would probably fall asleep without coming out of their room. They would never know I was gone. I grabbed a sweatshirt and headed out.

Aaron was on the corner with Dobie and a big dude who introduced himself as Ox.

"The best offensive linemen in Pilchuck," Aaron said.

We all slapped hands.

I tried to make eye contact with Dobie, but he was looking down or at Aaron. I wondered if Aaron had texted Dobie right before me, or if they had planned this together. I noticed that Aaron and Dobie were each clutching large brown paper bags in their hands, which also seemed odd.

"So, what are we doing?" I asked.

"We're going to play a game," Aaron answered. "It's called 'blind as a bat.' Don't worry, it's not dangerous."

"How come it's just us?" I asked.

"Too many people draws a crowd," Aaron explained.

"Okay," I said. "What do we do?"

Ox looked at me. "Not *we*, freshman. You."

"We've all done it," Aaron assured me.

"Cool," I said, feeling pretty relaxed. It was obviously a tradition. And, besides, what could be worse than jumping off the Verlot Street bridge? "What do I do?"

"You two are going to complete three simple challenges," Aaron explained. "First, climb the fence at Boardman Park. Second, hit a baseball."

That doesn't sound too hard, I thought.

"Wearing these," Ox said, holding out two dark hoods.

Aaron gestured to the hoods. "Put them on."

A second later the world went black.

"Ready?" Aaron asked.

"Ready," Dobie replied.

"Yeah," I said as they began to lead me down the street. "Hey, what's the third thing?"

"Just a delivery," Aaron replied. "Relax," he added. "This will be fun. I promise."

Aaron and Ox made Dobie and me make up raps about each other as we walked. Something about the way Dobie rhymed *McCleary* with *smeary* and *teary* made us all crack up. Then they all busted on me because I couldn't think of anything that rhymed with *Dobie*. We were laughing so hard, I forgot I was blindfolded. I was stoked about having friends like these in high school.

After a few blocks, I could tell we were in Boardman Park. There was no mistaking the smell of the grass and the sounds of the swings creaking in the breeze.

"Reach out," Aaron ordered.

I stuck my hands out and felt the cool metal of the fence that ran along the first-base line of the ball field.

"Start climbing," Ox said.

Scaling the fence in the dark was not especially scary or hard, even if I couldn't see anything. It shook a little, especially with the two of us climbing side by side. And I had to find my balance at the top before I swung my legs over and started down. Above me I heard the sound of Dobie's pants ripping, which killed Aaron and Ox and almost made me fall. Otherwise it was easy. We were back on the ground in less than a minute.

One down. Two to go.

Hitting a baseball in the dark was harder.

Ox pitched from the mound. "Ready?" he asked.

"Ready," I said. I heard the sound of his foot dragging across the dirt, then swung a couple of seconds later. Whiff. The ball smacked the backboard. Aaron and Ox laughed.

"Little early," Aaron said.

I didn't make contact on the next three either. According to Aaron I was too high, too low, then too late. I got a piece of the fifth pitch, which meant I was getting the timing. After three more tries, I finally made solid contact, slapping a ball toward the right side of the infield—at least that was what it felt like. Dobie went next, taking about as long as I did to knock out a legitimate hit.

Two down. One to go.

"Nicely done, boys," Aaron said. "You guys have legitimate talent. It's going to be great having you on the team."

"Thanks, man," I replied, trying to hold on to the memory of this so I could share it with Charlie. He'd eat this up.

"What's next?" Dobie asked.

"This way," Ox said.

After another ten minutes of walking and rapping, I was pretty turned around. But my gut told me we were back on my street. The cracks in the sidewalk felt familiar. We stopped, and Aaron shoved what felt like one of the paper bags into my hands. Whatever was in it was soft and not very heavy. I wasn't sweating it. This night was too great to worry about anything.

Aaron's voice broke the silence. "Delivery time."

Dobie went first. "Can I take my hood off?" he asked.

"Go for it," Aaron answered.

Next I heard footsteps moving away. Then came the sound of a doorbell. I picked up muffled conversation. It all seemed friendly. The door closed, and a few seconds later Dobie returned.

We went a little farther.

"Your turn, McCleary," Aaron said. "Take the hood off."

It took me a moment as my eyes adjusted to the darkness. When I got my bearings, I realized we were in front of Tessa's house. "What are we doing here?" I asked.

"Making a delivery," Aaron said with a smile.

I glanced at Dobie. Again, he avoided eye contact. Nobody was laughing or rapping anymore.

"Go ahead," Ox said, pointing to the door.

"What's in the bag?" I asked.

"That's a surprise," Aaron answered.

"It's nothing illegal," Ox promised.

Knowing it wasn't illegal didn't make me feel better. I could do the math. Aaron didn't like Tessa. There was zero chance that whatever was in the bag was something she would want. But what choice did I have? I would never live it down if I wimped out now. My only option was to go through with it and explain the whole thing to Tessa later. She'd get it.

So I rang her doorbell.

Tessa answered. She was wearing sweatpants and a T-shirt. Oreo appeared at my feet and pawed my leg. "Hey," Tessa said, sounding surprised. From her angle, there was no way she could see Aaron, Ox, and Dobie. "What are you doing here?"

"I don't know what's in here," I said. "But I have to give it to you. It's kind of a dare."

"Oh-kay," Tessa said, taking the bag. "Do you want me to open it now?"

"I guess so," I said quietly, feeling the dread rising from my core.

Tessa opened the brown paper bag and reached inside. What she pulled out was the worst thing, besides maybe a human head, I could have imagined.

Aaron Parker was evil.

CHAPTER THIRTY-SEVEN

→ TESSA

A cheerleading uniform. Green and white, with yellow trim. That was what was in the bag. I clenched it with a fury I had never known before. I was angry and humiliated, and even more than that, hurt.

"Is this a joke?" I asked Caleb, trying not to let any tears leak from my eyes.

He shook his head. "I had to," he said.

I ignored Caleb's pitiful answer. "Is that what you see when you look at me?" I asked, shoving the skirt and top into his hands. "A cheerleader? Is that what you want—me jumping up and down on the sideline, waiting for you after the game? Because that's not going to happen. That's not who I am. And if you don't get that by now, I don't want to be your friend or your girlfriend or your anything."

"No," he said. "That's not it. I just—it's a thing they made me do."

I had no idea who Caleb was talking about, and I didn't

care. He had walked up to my door with his own two feet and handed me that bag. Everything he did was all on him. "You know what, Caleb?" I said, before I slammed the door. "If you're going to be a jerk, at least own it."

I made up my mind right then that I was not going to lie down on my bed and cry myself to sleep. I was the football girl. And the football girl did not get sad. She got even. I cornered Mom and Dad in the kitchen.

"Phones down," I said. "We have to talk."

They laid down their phones. "What's the matter?" Mom asked.

"I want to go to that football camp," I said. "I'm not taking no for an answer."

"That's an exaggeration," Dad said.

"Tessa," Mom asked, "what does be afraid mean?"

"It was just talk," I said. "I was sending a message. But now I mean it."

"What exactly is the message?" Dad asked.

Did I really have to explain it? For two people running a political campaign, these two could be surprisingly dense. "The message is that I'm not afraid."

"And now you need to back it up," Mom said.

"Yes!" I answered gratefully. I handed her the permission form. "All you need to do is sign this."

Mom scanned the sheet of paper. "This is two weeks, every weekday, all day."

"I know."

"What about the campaign?" Dad asked.

"I was thinking I could take a break," I said. "You've got, like, a million volunteers. Please. It would make a great story. We could call Beth. It could help you."

Mom and Dad looked at each other. In that moment, I wondered whether they were my parents or two people trying to win an election. I knew I was right. This would be on the front page of the newspaper. And the truth was, I didn't really care anymore if I was the football girl or just a girl playing football. I wanted to show everyone I could go through with it.

"You understand my concerns," Mom said.

"Yes."

"Tell me."

"You think it's dangerous. You think I might not even play. Which is kind of a contradiction. But I'm okay with it. You think I'll be a social outcast. You think if I do well in football camp, I'll try out for the team and make it and it'll take over my life and I'll flunk all my classes because I'll spend all my time studying my playbook, which I won't need, since I won't play anyway."

"Most of that is true," Mom said. "But can I say one more thing?"

"Okay."

"It doesn't seem like very long ago that you were excited about cross-country. You received a medal. You and Marina and Lexie were ready to join the team together. I was very happy for you."

Mom stopped talking. I think it was a politician's trick.

She was daring me to agree with her or tell her she was wrong. But everything she had said was true. For a second, I traveled back in time and relived that afternoon. Part of me wished that was how it had gone. That I had finished the flag football season and called it quits. That I had caught the game-winning pass. Or that Caleb hadn't made me believe I was legit, or that I'd kept my mouth shut during that first interview with Beth. I could have spent all summer running with Lexie and Marina and hung out with Caleb in my free time, instead of mixing everything up. Too bad that wasn't the way it had played out. I had to take this one step further. Cross-country would always be there.

"Why didn't you tell me you were happy for me?" I asked.

"I don't remember what I said," Mom admitted.

"You told me you were running for mayor."

Mom sighed and looked at the permission form. "I'm still not sure about this."

Dad reached across the table and gently took the paper. He picked up a pen and signed the form. "I am," he said.

"Alan," Mom said, "we need to talk about this."

"Tessa has made her case," Dad said. "I trust her. I think you do too."

After a long pause, Mom kissed me on the cheek. "Okay," she said. Then she signed the form too.

CHAPTER THIRTY-EIGHT

→ CALEB

I stood on the Dooleys' front porch trying to figure out my next move. There was no point knocking or texting. Tessa would ignore me. I looked down at the cheerleading uniform in my hands. It was the only thing I had. How could I have been so dumb? What had I thought her reaction was going to be? There had to be some way I could make Tessa see that I was sorry. More than sorry, that I was a fool for letting Aaron Parker do what he'd done. And I was a fool for having followed through with it. An idea hit me. It would be brutal. But it might work.

Aaron, Ox, and Dobie must have left during my heated conversation with Tessa, because when I headed back to the street, it was empty. As I walked home, I tried to psych myself up. I would go through with it. I owed Tessa that.

THURSDAY, JULY 14

In the morning I came down to the kitchen wearing baggy sweatpants and a loose hoodie. Dad was sipping coffee and reading the paper. I saw him watch me cross the room.

"You all right, Caleb?" he asked.

"I'm fine. Why?"

"You look a little stiff. Did you pull something?"

"I might have," I said. "I played football with some of the guys from the baseball team the other day. I think I tweaked my hamstring. I'll walk it off."

"You're young," Dad replied. "You'll get over it." He went back to the paper. I didn't think he had any clue what I had on underneath my sweats.

I ducked out the back door and jogged down to Board-man Park. It was nine-thirty. I knew that most days Tessa went running in the morning with Marina and Lexie. I was taking a chance.

The park was still quiet. I walked across the dewy grass to the end of the trail the girls liked to run. I took off my pants and sweatshirt. And I waited.

I wasn't sure exactly what the people who came along thought when they saw me. They probably figured I was out of my mind. Then again, I was standing in the middle of the park in an outfit that only covered half my body, so I couldn't really blame them. I actually got used to the stares. It was the breeze that bothered me. Also, parts of me were itching. I was about to give up when I saw three pairs of running shoes emerge from the woods.

Tessa sprinted to the end of the trail, slowed up, and then stopped and put her hands on her knees. She was sweating and bright red. Marina saw me first. She put her hand over her mouth and leaned into Lexie, who turned around, hiding her head. Tessa finally lifted her eyes in my direction.

I didn't speak or move. Even when the light breeze blew the cheerleading skirt up, I was a statue. I had no idea what would happen next, but I knew there was no way Tessa could ignore me.

"Oh my God, Caleb," she said, sounding amused and angry at the same time. "What are you doing?"

My next move was not planned. It just came to me. I rolled my arms one over the other in front of me, waved my hands, and then finished with a bow. "Spirit hands!" I said.

"I think you mean *spirit fingers*," Marina replied.

"Spirit fingers," I said back, waving my hands again.

Lexie shook her head. "I can't watch this. I am too embarrassed for everyone here."

Tessa walked toward me. She pointed to my clothes on the ground. "Please put those on. Now."

"No, not until I say this. I'm sorry. What I did was really stupid, and I really, really feel bad about it. I wasn't thinking. When I look at you, the last thing I see is a cheerleader."

"Try again," Lexie said.

"I mean, if you wanted to be a cheerleader, great. But you should do what you want to do. If you want to play football, play football. Who cares what anyone thinks?"

"What do *you* think?" Tessa asked.

"You should do whatever you want," I said. "And you should say you forgive me, because I will never do anything that dumb again for as long as you know me."

CHAPTER THIRTY-NINE

→TESSA

THURSDAY, JULY 14

How was I supposed to stay mad at Caleb? Sure, he looked like a cheerleading werewolf. But he was the sorriest, and cutest, cheerleading werewolf ever.

"I forgive you," I said.

CHAPTER FORTY

→ CALEB

SUNDAY, JULY 17

On the afternoon before football camp, Tessa and I climbed to the ridge. We hadn't been there since we'd had our picture taken—the one that had ended up in the paper.

"I have to tell you something," Tessa said when we reached the top. "I'm going to camp tomorrow. My parents signed the form. I didn't want you to be surprised, even though I figured you already knew, and please do not try to talk me out of it."

"Why would I do that?"

"Are you serious? I know nobody else on the team wants me there."

"Well, I do," I said.

"They'll hate you."

"Maybe a few of them will. But Charlie says winning fixes everything. I wasn't sure what that meant. Now I think I do."

"What do you think will happen?" Tessa asked.

In all my conversations with Tessa, I had tried to be honest with her. Not just because I was a terrible liar. I wanted her to know that I thought she was a good football player. And I also wanted her to know that most guys would have a major problem with a girl on the team. Now I had to be honest with her one more time.

"I think you'll hate it," I said. "It's not like football in the park. We're going to have gear on. The coaches will be yelling at us. People are going to hit you. We'll be running, a lot. Actually, you might like that part. But except for that, I think you're going to wish you were on a trail somewhere."

"If it's so awful, why are you doing it?" Tessa asked.

"Because I think I can be the next quarterback," I said. "Not this year. Maybe not even next year, but eventually. And then all the work and all the suffering will be worth it. That's what matters to me."

There was more to it. I wanted to be the next McCleary to play for Pilchuck High School. To be a star, just like my big brother, Charlie, who had followed in my dad's footsteps. Who knew what would happen after that? Maybe I would help run the family business, and maybe I wouldn't. But if I didn't, I was certain now that my dad wouldn't have the same reaction he'd had when Charlie had wanted to do his own thing, have his own career.

Tessa was quiet. I wondered what mattered to her. Did she want to start on the varsity team like me? It wasn't impossible. There were small receivers in the league. But they were obsessed with football—more than Tessa. I remembered guys

Charlie had hung out with in high school. They geeked out on memorizing fades and slants and whip routes and figuring out how to beat bigger corners, and they could take a hit. They put in their time on special teams because they all thought they could play in college or in the pros. Being great was what mattered to them. I wasn't sure it was the same for Tessa. But I knew she had made up her mind about this. And so had I. If it was important to her, it didn't matter what the reason was. It was important to me too.

"You do have one problem," I said.

"What's that?"

"You can't show up tomorrow in running shoes and a T-shirt."

Chapter Forty-One

→TESSA

MONDAY, JULY 18

I was jealous of Caleb. Not because he might get what he needed from football. But because he knew what he wanted. He had the next four years of his life planned out. Football camp was just a step on the way to a spot on the team, just like flag football had been a step toward camp. He wasn't trying to just survive the first day or prove that he belonged. He had dreams.

What was my dream? I was still trying to figure that out as Mom drove me to the high school. I'd be happy if I could figure out how to put on my shoulder pads the right way. What I really wanted was the chance to make one great play.

When we got out of the car, I could see that there were already boys everywhere. Fifty, a hundred maybe, some in gym shorts, some in football pants, all in jerseys and shoulder pads. Most wore helmets, and if not, there was one at their feet. They stood in small groups, laughing and pushing each other around, or running simple two-on-one drills. I counted seven coaches marching in between the boys—clapping, shouting, and writing secret notes on clipboards. I was a small fish swimming into a shark tank. All by choice. Just to prove I could.

I paused in the parking lot, waiting for Mom to ask me if I was sure. But she led the way, right up to the registration table.

"Go ahead," she said.

The man sitting behind the table was wearing sunglasses. He glanced up at Mom, then back to me. "Hi," he said, like we might be there to ask for directions to some other camp.

"I'd like to sign up," I managed to say.

"For football camp?" he asked.

I nodded. "My name is Tessa Dooley." I handed him the permission slip.

"Oh, I know who you are," he replied, taking my form. He studied it for a minute. "Is she with you too?" he asked.

"She's my mom."

The man looked up. "No. Her." I followed his gaze and spotted Beth on the other side of the field. She was talking to one of the coaches.

"What's Beth doing here?" I asked Mom.

"I didn't call her."

"Then who did?"

"She's a reporter, Tessa. She's writing a story. That's her job."

"Sorry," I said.

Mom smiled. "You just go out there and do your best. And try to pretend the whole town isn't watching."

"Is that what you do?"

"Either that or I picture everyone naked."

My eyes swept across the field. "Gross."

CHAPTER FORTY-TWO
→ CALEB

Dobie, Nick, and I were playing catch near the bleachers when Tessa arrived. Some of the other guys were stretching. The coaches were in the middle of the field looking at clipboards. In a few minutes they were going to check us in.

I caught a pass from Nick, pivoted, got my feet set, and rifled the ball to Dobie. There was a whap as it hit his hands.

"Hey!" he said. "What's with the heat?"

"Sorry, dude," I answered. "Just a little jacked I guess."

It was all happening. No more peewee games. No more flag football. No more two-hand touch. We were in the big leagues now. I knew it wasn't going to be easy. I was going to get hit, bruised, and yelled at like a pig. But it was going to make me a man, the same way it had made Charlie a man and Dad a man. Plus, it was going to be fun. The uniforms. The lights. All we needed were cheerleaders.

Nick was about to throw to Dobie. I saw him pause in

the middle of his motion. He dropped his arm just as his eyes found Tessa walking toward the coaches.

Dobie glared at me. "If you don't go over there and tell her to go home, I will."

"Why would you do that?"

"Why would you do that?" Dobie snarled. "Because if you don't, those guys will make sure you never play football again, and you'll take us down with you, and that's not going to happen."

I looked over at Nick.

"Just do it nicely," he said with a shrug.

I walked away from them. I had to think for myself. I blocked out all the other voices. I went straight to Aaron Parker. He and some of the other older players were there as assistant coaches. Aaron was twirling a whistle on a string.

"Parker," I said, coming up from behind.

"That's me," he said, turning around. He started to smile. Then he saw Tessa. "Why is she here?"

"She's not leaving, dude. You got it? She has a right to be here."

"You're making a mistake," Aaron answered quietly. "I've been cool to you because your brother was cool to me, but I am telling you now, this is my team. I do not want her here. She's poison."

"She's a football player."

"Don't make me laugh."

"She's a football player," I repeated.

"You know I'm a captain, right?" Aaron asked. "That means Coach cares what I think about who makes the team.

He'll ask me after camp who I liked. I'll name a few guys. And they're in. And the rest," he said, pointing to the parking lot, "can go join the chess team."

I knew that was not exactly how it worked. There was no way the coaches would let a player—even a captain—decide who made the team. So, the threat didn't really scare me, although I knew Aaron could easily make my life miserable as long as we were in the same school, and maybe afterward too. But I couldn't back down now. That would be even worse.

"You said it yourself," I replied. "Someday this team is going to need me. And when I'm picking my nose in drama club instead of helping us win, everyone's going to know it's because of you, because you couldn't handle one girl in football camp. So get over it."

"Wow, that's big talk for a freshman," Aaron said. "Even a McCleary. You better be ready to prove it. Or I am going to make this the longest year of your life."

After he walked away, Dobie and Nick came up to me.

"What did you do?" Dobie asked.

"I think I just painted a bull's-eye on my butt."

CHAPTER FORTY-THREE

→ TESSA

I had never worn a football helmet. I had worn bike helmets, ski helmets, and a hockey mask for Halloween. But this was different. The first thing I wondered, after my first few breaths, was how many people had stunk up this helmet before me. As I ran wind sprints in the baking sun, I could feel my skull absorbing the stench of a thousand sweaty freshmen.

All I could see was the world straight ahead of me. Caleb could have been right at my side, and I wouldn't have known. So I focused on the white line at the other end of the field, and when I got there, I turned around and did it again.

That was the first day of football camp.

One down. Nine to go.

"So you didn't even play football?" Marina asked me later that day as we sat by the public pool.

"We just ran," I groaned. I wasn't even going to pretend I had enjoyed it. My friends would have seen through the act anyway. "My head still hurts from the helmet. I think it was too tight."

"We ran too," Lexie said, rubbing it in. "Of course all I felt was the cool breeze on my cheeks as we sprinted through the forest."

"Are you going back?" Marina asked.

"Yes," I replied. "I have to do something great."

"Here we go again," Marina said.

"Nah, it's not like that anymore," I replied. "I don't mean catching a game-winning pass. I already know that's probably not going to happen."

"Well, what, then?" Lexie asked.

"I haven't figured it out."

"You could *not* die," Marina suggested. "That would be great."

"I would settle for that," I answered.

"Well, if you do survive, you can always come running back to us," Lexie said. "We'll only make you feel bad for the rest of your life."

"Promise?"

Lexie spit into her palm and held out her hand. "Promise," she said.

"Ugh," I groaned, before cracking up. "You're worse than the boys."

After jumping into the pool to bathe in chlorine, I said goodbye to Marina and Lexie and walked stiffly home in the late afternoon heat. Knowing we would be friends, no matter what, took a lot of the sting out of the first day of football camp. It would take more than one rough day to get me off the football field.

I had gone a few blocks when Caleb texted me.

Frozen yogurt?

Can't walk that far.

K. BTW, Charlie says second day's the hardest.

Hate u.;)

CHAPTER FORTY-FOUR

→ CALEB

TUESDAY, JULY 19

The second day of football camp had barely started when Aaron found me.

"You come with me," he said.

"What do you mean?" I asked. "We're about to run lines."

"Not you," he said. "I have a special activity for you." He pointed to the stairs that ran up the side of the stands.

Aaron owned me, and we both knew it. I had jumped off a bridge for him. There was no question that I would run stairs. So, whenever the whistle blew, the rest of the guys—and Tessa—sprinted across the field, while I dashed up the stairs. It was my punishment, and I had to take it. I realized something else: Aaron had become so obsessed with teaching me a lesson that he'd forgotten about Tessa. Maybe that was also because when the helmets went on, nobody seemed to care that there was a girl on the field. It was starting to look like whatever Aaron had been afraid of was mostly inside his own head.

During a water break, Aaron pulled me to the side. "I want to show you something," he said. "You see those helmets?"

On the equipment bench, there were six helmets lined up.

"Yeah," I panted.

"Yesterday there were people wearing those helmets. Do you know what happened to those people?"

"They quit."

Aaron nodded. "They couldn't handle it. And I'm going to make sure the next helmet up there is yours."

Just then one of the coaches yelled over to Aaron. I exhaled in relief. Someone was coming to my rescue. "Parker!" I heard the coach yell. "Why isn't that camper doing push-ups?"

"Sorry, sir," Aaron answered. "I'll make him do double for slacking."

"Double?"

"Eat dirt," Aaron said, pointing to the ground.

The only good thing that happened on the second day was that Tessa stopped being the football girl. I didn't hear one person say a word about a girl being on the field. It was the opposite of everything I'd expected. Aaron had made me believe the whole team would go berserk if a girl showed up for football camp. But he was wrong. I think it helped that we were suffering, and that Tessa was feeling the pain right beside us.

"Gotta hand it to you," Dobie said to Tessa as she sat on

the bleachers at the end of the day. "You're tougher than I thought."

"So are you," Tessa said to Dobie.

"Shut up, Tessa," Dobie said, wiping his forehead off with a dirty towel.

I smiled at Tessa, who managed to laugh. I hoped she realized that *shut up* was Dobie's way of saying *You're pretty cool.*

After dinner that night I called Charlie and told him how Aaron had made me run stairs.

"Classic," Charlie said. "I wonder where he learned that."

"What are you saying?" I asked, sensing that Charlie was being sarcastic.

"I'm saying I did the same thing to him three years ago."

"Why?"

"When you're a senior and you get attitude from a freshman, you have to put him in his place. That was my job. It gave me no pleasure."

"Liar."

"Yeah," Charlie said with a laugh. "I loved it. And so will you."

"Running stairs?"

"No, making some other punk run stairs."

"Never," I said.

"That's what I thought," Charlie replied. "But it happened."

"You're saying I'm going to turn into Aaron Parker? Kill me now."

"Hey, Aaron is Aaron. But he's a captain. And he's earned it. You have to respect that."

"Doesn't mean I want to be him."

"Doesn't mean you have to. You be the man you want to be. But my money says you'll be in his shoes someday."

"Because I'm a McCleary?"

"Because you're Caleb."

CHAPTER FORTY-FIVE
→ TESSA

THURSDAY, JULY 21

On the fourth day of camp, the coaches broke us into groups.
First we were divided into offense and defense. Then they
split the offense into receivers and backs.

That was how I ended up in a small group standing
around a tall, thin coach who clapped at some point during
every sentence and walked with a slight limp. He told us his
name was Coach St. James.

"You guys ready?" he asked.

CLAP.

"Yeah," a couple of us responded.

"I didn't hear that."

CLAP.

"Yes, sir!" we all shouted.

"That's better. Now . . ." CLAP. "Who's played receiver before?"

Four people raised a hand. Three didn't.

Coach St. James looked at the three of us who had not raised our hands. "Never?" he asked, like we might be lying. He walked up to me. "You've never caught a football?"

"Just in pickup games and flag football," I said.

"Well, that counts. Raise your hand, football girl!"

I raised my hand.

"What about you two?" Coach St. James asked with a clap as he faced the boys who had not raised their hands. "Are you telling me that in your entire lives nobody has ever thrown a football in your general direction?"

Both boys raised their hands.

CLAP.

"Well then," Coach St. James said. "You are all wide receivers. I'm not saying you're good wide receivers. I'm not saying you'll ever play wide receiver for Pilchuck High School or any other high school. For all I know you might have bricks for hands and the acceleration of one-legged dogs. But for now, you are wide receivers." CLAP. "Can we agree on that?"

We all nodded. Deep inside my dark and stinky helmet, I was smiling because someone who didn't know me was saying I had the same chance as anyone else on the field. He didn't care who I was, just that I had two hands and two legs and knew which way to run. At last I wasn't the football girl. I was a wide receiver. Maybe not a good one. But that was what I was.

"Marvelous!" Coach St. James said. "Let's talk about footwork!"

CLAP.

Beth found me after camp while I was waiting for Caleb. She approached me slowly. "Your mom said it was okay if we talked. If you're up for it."

"Sure. What do you want to talk about?"

"Well, for starters, are you having fun?"

"I'm not sure I'd say that."

"What would you say?"

"I'd say I'm learning a lot."

"Like what?"

"Like nobody really cares that I'm a girl."

"The last time we spoke, you said the boys should be afraid. Do you think they're afraid of you?"

"I think that was a dumb thing to say."

"I loved it," Beth said. "How did the boys take it?"

"I think they kind of forgot about me," I said.

"Is that a good thing?"

"Yes. It's a good thing. I mean, part of me liked the attention. But this was never about trying to make some big statement about how girls can play football too. Lots of girls have played football already, so who am I to act like this is some huge courageous thing I'm doing?"

"What is it about?"

"It seems stupid now," I said.

"If it feels stupid after you tell me, I promise I'll forget you ever said it."

I told Beth about the end of the championship game.

"You need a win," she said.

"Well, we're not even playing games, so . . ."

Beth shook her head. "Sorry, I don't mean a win like winning a game. I mean a win like something happening that you'd feel good about. It's an expression."

"Yeah," I agreed. "When you put it that way, I need a win."

"Is proving the boys wrong a win?"

"Kind of," I said. "But what's so great about proving someone else wrong when they don't really care that much anyway?"

"That's a good question," Beth sighed. "To be honest, I'm trying to figure out if this story is even a story. Or maybe the story is that it's not a story." She paused and looked at me. "But that doesn't mean it's not important. You're doing something you wanted to do—something you're good at—even when you were told not to. You'll have that forever, no matter what else happens."

"Thank you," I said, loving the praise. "Are you going to write about this?" I asked.

Beth nodded. "It'll be in the paper next week."

"Do you know what the headline will be?"

"What do you think it should be?"

"How about FOOTBALL HELMETS, SOURCE OF ALL HUMAN DISEASES?"

Beth laughed. "Maybe that's the story here."

Neither of us had to say that one of the people who'd told me not to play football was my mom, Councilwoman Dooley. In my heart, I believed that Beth knew that what happened between the football girl and her mother was nobody's business, and we needed to figure out our own issues outside of the media.

Chapter Forty-Six

→ CALEB

FRIDAY, JULY 22

"Can I ask you something?" Tessa said as we walked slowly home from football camp.

"Not if it's about running stairs," I replied, feeling the ache in my legs.

"It's not that," Tessa said, letting go of my hand long enough to slap at a mosquito on her arm. "If I told you 'I need a win,' what would you think I meant?"

"You need to win what?" Caleb asked.

Tessa smiled at me like I had done her a favor. "See, that's what I would have said too. Beth—you know, the reporter—said I need *a* win. Not like a game, though. Just something good that happens."

"Like what?"

"I don't know. What would it be for you?"

"Something good that happens at football camp?"

187

"Yeah, and it has to be something you do, not just something that happens."

Secretly I thought standing up to Aaron might have been my win, even though I was paying a price for it. That felt bigger than any play or throw I could make in a scrimmage. I thought that was what Charlie would have said too. I just wasn't sure how to explain it all to Tessa. "How about not puking all over my shoes on the first day?" I said.

"I really like my coach," Tessa said, almost to herself.

"St. James? Yeah, I know him. He's cool. He was a wide receiver in college. He played in the Rose Bowl."

"I wonder what he thinks of me."

"We're pretty much all numbers to them," I said.

"Then I hope when he thinks of number eighty-three, he doesn't remember that I'm a girl."

We walked another block without talking. There were so many things I could have told Tessa about football camp. I wanted her to know that I was killing it in the quarterback drills. I wanted to tell her that I thought having a girlfriend in football camp was weirdly awesome. And I wanted to give her the bad news, that it was easy to forget she was a girl during wind sprints and no-contact drills. It would be a lot harder next week when we actually started hitting each other.

"I hope my coach doesn't forget I'm not a girl," I said.

Tessa squeezed my hand. "You're twisted."

Chapter Forty-Seven

→ TESSA

TUESDAY, JULY 26

I learned one thing during the second week. Getting tackled hurts badly. Almost as badly as having to admit that everyone who warned me was right.

The first hit happened late on Tuesday. The play was a slant route. Ten steps, then break left. Five steps, then turn and catch. I got a great break off the line of scrimmage, just like Coach St. James had taught me, ran my pattern perfectly, and raised my hands at the moment the ball was in the air. It was a clean catch and I tucked the ball away.

Then.

Lights out.

I don't know who hit me. He was big and moving fast. I think it's what falling off a bridge onto concrete and getting run over by a fully loaded dump truck would feel like.

The impact was somewhere between my lower back and my side.

I lay in the dirt, staring up at the clouds, clenching my eye muscles to hold in the tears. I remembered how Caleb had warned me that no guy would ever tackle a girl because the guy wouldn't want to hurt her. So far, that was not my experience. Whoever had just hit me did not seem very concerned with my health. I got to my feet and faked a steady walk back to the huddle.

Coach St. James blew his whistle. "Let's take five," he said.

Someone reminded him that we had just taken a break.

"I don't care," Coach replied.

During the break, he looked at me and raised a thumb. I could tell it was a question. I raised my thumb back.

It was a lie.

I was still hurting that night. The pain was soul crushing in the biggest way. Not because I couldn't take it, but because I knew I didn't want to. I had to admit to myself that any sport that did this to my body was not for me. In fact, I wasn't sure anybody should play a sport that did this to them. I wasn't going to quit camp. I was going to take a hundred more hits before the week was done. But I knew 100 percent in that moment that my idea of playing football in high school was over.

Some win.

CHAPTER FORTY-EIGHT
↳ CALEB

THURSDAY, JULY 28

By the end of the second week, the coaches had sorted us into an A team and a B team. They didn't say it, but I knew what it meant. The players on the A team had a chance to be on the varsity team in the fall. Everyone else would be JV. Nick and I were on the A team. Dobie and Tessa were on the B team. On the last day of camp, the two teams were going to play each other in a scrimmage—pads, helmets, tackling, everything. It might get fierce because there was a chance any of us could move up if we played well, or move down if we choked.

"I'm coming for you tomorrow, McCleary," Dobie said as we stretched on the field the day before the game.

"I'm shaking," I said.

"And you'll have to go through me," Nick answered.

While Nick and Dobie went at each other, I watched

Tessa come out of the girls' locker room wearing football pants, a jersey, and shoulder pads. She waved to the other receivers, then found a spot on the grass by herself.

I jogged over to her. "Last day," I said. "You ready for the scrimmage tomorrow?"

Tessa sat down, extended her leg out in front of her, leaned over her knee, and reached for her toes. "I guess," she said, in a voice I knew by now meant *I'm acting like there's something wrong and I don't want to talk about it, except I really do.*

I sat down a few feet away from her. "Are you nervous? It's not that big a deal. It's just a scrimmage."

"That's just it," she said. "It's just a scrimmage. I've been here for almost two weeks, and I haven't done anything, nothing anybody will ever be impressed by."

"It's just football camp. I don't think ESPN is coming."

Tessa sat up and glared at me. "Shut up. You're not funny."

"Okay, but all I'm saying is, nobody here has done anything that great. We're all running and doing drills, and that's about it. The highlights come later, when the season starts."

"What if I don't make it that far?"

"What do you mean? You'll make JV."

Tessa shook her head. "That's not what I'm saying. I'm not sure I want to play high school football. In fact, I'm pretty sure I don't."

Tricky situation. I could have either acted really surprised even though I wasn't, or acted like I wasn't surprised, which would basically have been like telling Tessa *I told you so.* The one thing I could not do was tell Tessa that I was relieved. I genuinely believed she *could* be on the football team, and I thought she had a right to be on the football team. But if I was being totally honest, I would say that I really, really didn't want Tessa to be on the football team, and I was sure there was no guy on earth who would have felt any differently if he'd been in my shoes.

"All I can say is, it's awesome that you were here. I'll remember it."

CHAPTER FORTY-NINE

→TESSA

It was one of the nicest things anyone had ever said to me, and it was even better because it was the truth. Caleb hadn't been trying to cheer me up. He'd just said it because that was what he thought. He probably didn't even realize how much his words meant to me. I was tempted to write a note telling him. First, though, I wanted to destroy him on the football field.

I woke up on the last day of camp and immediately started doing jumping jacks in my room. I shadowboxed in front of the mirror. I did push-ups until my arms gave out. Then I went to the kitchen, pounded the water bottle I'd put in the fridge the night before, refilled it, and drained it again.

After that I belched so loudly, it woke my parents.

"Are you feeling all right?" Mom said over breakfast. "It sounded like you were getting sick earlier."

"Oh, that was just the garbage disposal," I said. "I'm fine. Ready for football."

"So are we," Dad answered as he spread cream cheese on a toasted bagel.

"What do you mean?"

"We're coming to your game," Mom said.

"It's not really a game," I answered. "And most of the people there won't be old enough to vote."

"I'm just going as your mother. Besides, things are quiet in the campaign. The general election isn't until November. I've got plenty of time to take down Joe Sterling."

"And a ten-point lead in the polls," Dad added.

"Unless you don't want us there," Mom said. "This is your day. I don't want to be a distraction."

My mom was making an effort. This was a small step, but I would take it. She was coming to watch *me*. Not the other way around.

"Mom."

"Yes?"

"Get over yourself."

There was a crowd at the field. Mom and Dad weren't the only ones who had come to watch. Caleb's family was there too—even Charlie, who was surrounded by a mob of older players in letterman jackets. I saw a group of younger girls sitting together in the front row of the bleachers, knocking back popcorn and pointing like they were at a real game. I had to take a deep breath and tell myself to relax. I wasn't expecting to be a hero or to do anything special. I just wanted to finish my tackle football career with dignity. Catch a few passes. Maybe haul in a touchdown. Embarrass the other team. Hug the opposing quarterback in front of all of his friends. Normal football stuff.

Coach St. James pulled us together before kickoff.

"I'm proud of all of you," he said. CLAP. Then he pointed to us one at a time. "You're football players." CLAP. "I hope you'll play for me this fall." CLAP. "Let's go get this done." CLAP.

We all clapped back.

After the game, I went to the girls' locker room. I sat on the bench and stared at the walls. In the other locker room, I could hear the boys shouting, laughing, banging lockers.

"I'll always have you," I said to my helmet.

Before I could help it, I was crying and smiling at the same time. Crying because I would never put on a helmet again, because I hated being alone in a locker room while everyone else was together, because I missed running with my friends and being a threesome of athletic power. And I was smiling because I had nothing to prove to anyone, especially myself. Even though I would have liked one highlight to end on.

The silence was broken by the locker room's metal door swinging open. Suddenly I was sharing the space with three girls—maybe fifth graders. They each had a bag of popcorn in their hands.

"Are you looking for the bathroom?" I asked.

One of them stepped forward. "My name is Kate Parker. Are you the football girl?" she asked.

"Her name is *Tessa*," one of Kate's friends whispered in disgust.

Kate spun around. "I *know* that, Julia," Kate shot back, hitting the *know* hard. "So, are you?" she asked me again.

"I'm Tessa," I said.

"Told you," said Julia.

Kate clenched her jaw but kept her eyes on me. "I just think . . . Well, we think you're really cool and it's awesome that you play football. My brother Aaron is on the football team, and I want to play too when I'm older."

I had to stop myself from saying, *Are you crazy?*

Here was this young girl telling me that her dream was to put on shoulder pads and a helmet and feel like she's getting hit by a wrecking ball for fun. To run sprints in the summer heat. To risk injury. To hear over and over again how football wasn't for girls. I wanted to tell her to join the swim team or Girl Scouts or anything besides football. Then I pictured her in four years with longer legs and muscles and bigger hands, and I got scared that whatever came out of my mouth now could be with her forever. What if she remembered me asking her *Are you crazy?* every time she wondered if she should try something new? There would be enough people saying that. She didn't need to hear it from me, the football girl, who she thought was really cool.

I knew then that this was the highlight I had been waiting for.

My win.

I handed Kate the helmet. "You want to try this on?" I asked.

Kate nodded. Her head disappeared into the helmet. But I could hear two words from behind the face mask. "This stinks!"

I smiled to myself and thought, *Get used to it.*

FAST AND FEARLESS,
THE FOOTBALL GIRL TAKES THE FIELD

Beth Meyer | Pilchuck Observer

There will be no record of the game played at Logger Field on Friday. It was a simple training scrimmage—a chance for boys with football dreams to put their new skills on display in front of coaches, older players, and family. Even the final score was in dispute. One coach guessed his team had won by a touchdown. Another thought it might have been a tie. Though it is hard to imagine two teams of highly competitive boys being content to play a game with no clear winner, the real surprise might be that not all of the players were boys.

Or is it?

When Tessa Dooley used a live television appearance to announce her intent to play organized football, it felt like the start of something momentous. How would the town react to this daring defiance of tradition? Even her own parents were uneasy with her ambitions.

"I always said that if I had a son, I would never let him play football," said her mother, Jane Dooley, the city councilwoman running for mayor. "But how could I hold my daughter back from crossing the same kind of invisible line that I've had to cross myself? What I learned is that it's more than a game."

Indeed, Tessa appears to have made history. There is no record of a girl suiting up for an official game of tackle football, at least in Pilchuck. Nationally, the number of girls playing high school football is small, but growing—more than 1,600 last year.

Don't bother Tessa with any of these numbers, though. "She never wanted to make history," says Caleb McCleary, 14, who identified himself as Tessa's boyfriend. "She just wanted to make a catch—and maybe the team." Caleb admitted there was resistance to the idea of Tessa being at camp. "There were a few guys who were worried she'd get hurt or that she'd be a distraction. But most of us were cool with it. I mean, it's the same deal with anyone. If you can play, you can play. My dad is kind of old-school, and even he had to give it up for Tessa in the end."

What does it take to convince a skeptic that a girl can hold her own on the football field? Here's one way: use a slick combination of speed and agility to lead the undersized B team with five catches, including three for first downs and one in the back of the end zone. Tessa did all that Friday on her way to a standing ovation, and, for good measure, she shook off a blistering hit and threw a few bone-crushing blocks of her own.

Tessa remains silent about her football future, declining to say whether she will try out for the high school team or return to cross-country running. "I guess what matters is that I have a choice," she says. "Whether I play football in high school or not, I'll never have to wonder what was possible. I came out, played hard, threw a mean block or two, and broke a few tackles. That's a win to me. I hope any girl who has the heart to play football will do the same."

ACKNOWLEDGMENTS

Thank you to Krista and Elizabeth for the guidance and support, and thanks most of all to my wife, Staci, for putting up with this writer for another book. KOTN.